Praise

"*My Life Crazy* paints a vivid picture of the lives of the majority of people in Central America. For those contemplating mission work, this is an excellent book to gain perspective on the reality of the systemic and cultural problems that pervade much of the third world and the need to show Christ's love to one person at a time in order to effect long-term changes."

– Ron Suarez, Chaplain and Short-term Missionary to Nicaragua

My Life Crazy

My Life Crazy

A Gringa's Life with the Salvadoran Gangs

by Kylla Hanson

TATE PUBLISHING & *Enterprises*

Published by Tate Publishing & Enterprises, LLC
127 E. Trade Center Terrace | Mustang, Oklahoma 73064 USA
1.888.361.9473 | www.tatepublishing.com

Tate Publishing is committed to excellence in the publishing industry. The company reflects the philosophy established by the founders, based on Psalm 68:11,
"The Lord gave the word and great was the company of those who published it."

Book design copyright © 2009 by Tate Publishing, LLC. All rights reserved.
Cover design by Tyler Evans
Interior design by Stefanie Rooney

Published in the United States of America

ISBN: 978-1-60696-149-0
1. Religion, Christian Ministry, Missions
2. Travel, Central America
09.01.27

Dedication

To Faith
Whom I love deeply
To those nearest and dearest to my heart
You know who you are
Y
Al Pueblo Salvadoreño
Con mucho respeto y cariño

Acknowledgments

There are many who have had a part in turning this book from just a file on my computer into a reality.

To the following I extend my heartfelt thanks: God, without a doubt, thank you so much for protecting me, sending me out to do really simple tasks that opened up many doors to your Word, and for loving me and using me in spite of my weaknesses and multiple flaws; Rachel May and Ricardo Sanchez, two brilliant professors, who instilled in me a fascination with Latin America and inspired me to go; my friends April and Lisa who first read the manuscript, in real time as I wrote it and gave their suggestions and advice ... I really needed that early encouragement; Kelli, Jennifer, Kelsey, Tammy, Cindy, Tania, Cathy, Connie, Karen, and Jennifer G., thanks for reading the finished product when I was scared to trust it and for becoming my cheerleaders; Mr. Tippit for writing the foreword and always being a part of the family, thank you.

Thanks to Tate Publishing for seeing the book as something that had potential, accepting my manuscript, and honoring Gato's memory; to all of my students and friends who, over the years, have listened to my stories about El Salvador and made me appreciate the memories all the more, I thank you.

To the congregation of Bethany Baptist Church and Lowell Bakke, who supported me both financially and through prayer while I was in El Salvador; thank you for all your support.

My family stood by me as I wrote this book even though it did make me moody to say the least. Their constant support helps sustain me. Mom and Jack, you have put your money where your mouth is when it comes to believing in me, and I really couldn't have done it without you. Cory, you gave me the space I needed to write this, and in spite of everything, you have remained the constant, loyal, good man I have always known, which makes you a truly incredible person. Faith, you are a constant joy, and I would definitely say that even with all the adventures I have had in life, being your mom has been the coolest thing I have ever had the privilege to experience. I am glad you got to meet Gato, and that he got to meet you.

Kirsta, Kendis, and Karin, I love you! You are always there when I need you; you're my favorite friends.

To my mom, who has been battered and bruised with me, as I have perpetually taken the road less traveled, thanks for putting up with me, loving me, and pulling me back to center more times than not.

To my dad, Ken, who didn't get to be here for this, but whom I know is proud, I love you, and this is as much for you as for anybody.

To the Salvadoran people, including my English students, the bus drivers on route 21, the vendors, my townspeople, the members of the Santo Tomas MS clique, Mejicanos MS clique, Parque Libertad 18th Street clique, and the gluesniffers, I extend a warm hug of thanks. Thank you for welcoming me into your country, for providing me with two of the best years of my life, and for being the surviving people you are. I respect and love you and your country very much. This book could not have been written without you.

And to my precious Gato, nunca te olvidaré. Te amo.

Foreword

By Sammy Tippit
International Evangelist, Christian Author,
and President of Sammy Tippit Ministries

Let me encourage you to sit down with Kylla Hanson and allow her to serve you a cup of coffee and tell her story. You will be spellbound by her dream and the journey to fulfill that dream. She will take you into the world of gangs in El Salvador, and you'll see them through the eyes of a loving God and a caring Christian. You will not only encounter their violence, but Kylla will take you beyond their brutality and expose their wounded hearts and deepest hurts.

This is the story of a courageous young woman who went where wounded people lived and showed God's love to them in a very practical way. Kylla shares the raw details of her journey to El Salvador. There's no sugarcoating of the facts, no sweeping of details under the carpet. She tells the story with a transparent and honest heart, including her joys, victories, and greatest disappointments.

There's no fairytale ending. No simplistic answers to life's difficult situations. What you discover in Kylla's story is a heart—one that longs to express Christ's love. Yet you won't find a super saint sharing her story. Rather, you'll come to know a real person who has experienced great pain and sorrow while trying to do that which is good and right. She will allow you to see her failures as well as her love for the gangs. You will be riveted by both.

But this story is not about Kylla. It's about the gangs of El Salvador—their needs, but most of all their hearts. One word of warning: by the time Kylla has finished telling you her story, you may want to take your coffee pot and serve someone in your community.

Introduction

I loved El Salvador. I had studied the politics of the region in college. I felt an affinity for its people before I even arrived there. They were a warrior people, having survived a bloody and heinously-fought civil war. They had survived oppression, injustice, and the intervention of the United States time and time again. I fell in love with the country before I knew it personally.

My research led me to read poems by Alfonso Quijada Urías about the Salvadoran experience during the war; novels like Claribel Alegria's *The Ashes of Izalco*, which explored the 1932 massacre of Salvadoran peasants seeking justice; and Manlio Argueta's *One Day of Life* in which he followed a woman through a day of her life surviving in the war-torn countryside.

Their words resonated with me. I wanted to know their El Salvador intimately. I longed to know Lupe from *One Day of Life* and have her tell me personally how it felt to struggle to survive. I yearned to hug the mother of Angelita Gómez who was searching for her "disappeared"[1] daughter in the poem "There's a Reward." I wanted to see Izalco and remember a time before I was born when people rose up for justice.

I wanted to walk the streets where Archbishop Oscar Romero[2] had walked and ministered valiantly to his beleaguered flock. I needed to visit the University of Central America (UCA) and see the rose garden which was planted in memory of the fallen Jesuit priests, their maid, and her daughter. I wanted to pay tribute to the massacred souls of El Mozote.[3] I wished to kiss the grave of Father Rutilio Grande, one of the first martyred for El Salvador's cause. I felt a compulsion to apologize to whomever would listen for having contributed to the devastation of this precious country through my own ignorance and bliss therein.

I wanted to ride in the brightly painted buses where people hung out the sides because there weren't enough seats. I wanted to hear the music of Salvadoran groups like Las Nenas del Grupo Caña and Jhose y Su Grupo Lora in person. I had contraband copies of videos from the region, and before I could even speak Spanish, I watched them to get a better idea of the country's culture.

I wanted to learn the language and wrap my head around the subtleties of their expressions. I wanted to give myself over to the land, learn from it, and be changed by it. I wanted to eat sopa de frijoles y tortillas a la Salvadoreña[4] in hundred-degree weather. I wanted to try a pupusa with tons of cortido[5] stuffed inside. I wanted to be as Salvadoran as is possible for a white girl living in Washington State.

The desire to be there burned inside me. I had to go and see the things I had read about. I wanted to meet with the FMLN[6] and hear them discuss agrarian reform. I wanted to drink the coffee grown in the mountains of the region. I wanted to walk the dock in La Libertad and smell the salty ocean wind mixed with fish and lobsters. And I wanted to know the people of this unbelievably strong country.

Even now, I am overwhelmed by emotion when I think of my adopted country. I can smell the mixture of corn masa and car exhaust blending with the sweet smell of the mangoes falling from the pregnant trees. I can hear women yelling, "Guineos, cinco al peso,"[7] while the microbus thunders by with salsa music blaring from its open windows. Everything is louder and more intense there. It is the most beautiful place.

And Gato is my El Salvador. He was from the moment I met him. All the sadness and brokenness of an existence begun in dire poverty, mixed with a fierce defiance against a world that had turned its back on him, was connected to this passionate yearning for life. He *was* El Salvador.

And when I think of him and see his face looking at me, so intent on communicating something for which he didn't have the words, I see my beloved El Salvador in all its glory and ugliness—its good and bad all jumbled together, an imperfect perfection.

When Gato died, a piece of *me* died. As cliché as that might sound, it is nonetheless true. I don't know when I will return there. I do not have the same compulsion I had before. I still love the country and honor it and the people who make it so special, but right now it is too painful to revisit.

I know I need to visit his grave. And I will. I need to tell him goodbye and let my tears blend with the tears of the others who have visited him in his final resting place. I need to buy as many roses as I can and place them at his head, so he knows I want him to see beauty even now. I need to say goodbye. I need him to know that I love him and miss him and that some days it feels like my broken heart has the power to crack apart my whole being.

Chapter 1

Juanes[8] is playing in the background, and I am no longer in my bedroom under the cozy blankets warming my freezing toes. I no longer feel the need to relax after a long day of work and errands. I am in El Salvador, hot and sweating. My hair is frizzy, and I am drinking cold water from a little plastic pouch to cool down and keep the dust from settling in my throat. I am waiting for the 21 bus to take me into San Salvador to visit friends. And I see him … my friend … the one whose memory is pulling me rather forcibly from my warm bed and current situation back into the tropical warmth, back into the world where I knew him, back into that magic land, and I want to cry.

Juanes sings his song, and the vision of my friend stands in front of me, taunting me because I cannot touch him even though he is right there. I cannot hear him even though he is talking. I cannot smell him. I cannot feel him. The song is the story of my friend even though Juanes wrote it for another. But I know Gato, and his story weighs on me now. My heart is tearing.

> *Tan fuerte fue su dolor que un día se lo llevó.*
> *Tan fuerte fue su dolor que su corazón se apagó.*
> *Tan fuerte fue su temor que un día solo lloró. Tan*
> *fuerte fue su temor que un día su luz se apagó.*[9]

I see him in the song's words. I hear his whistle, a distinct sound that tricks me into thinking he is nearby. But he is not nearby, and I feel betrayed by the sound that always made me smile. My Salvadoran friends didn't understand why I could always recognize Gato's whistle when no one else's ever impacted my memory. They laughed and teased me about him. Yet, though there was never a romantic love between Gato and me, a profound love did exist. It is something that I never could really explain to people. I don't know if Gato or I fully understood why we had the feelings we shared. They were fraternal and then some. They were pure in an impure world. However, I will not spend so much time explaining something inexplicable. It just *was*.

> *Juan preguntó por amor, y el mundo se lo negó. Juan preguntó por honor, y el mundo le dio deshonor. Juan pregunto por perdón, y el mundo lo lastimó. Juan preguntó y preguntó, y el mundo jamás lo escuchó.*[10]

I see him hanging halfway out of the bus as it pulls into the desvio[11] to pick up the customers. This is his habit, along with most other cobradores[12] in El Salvador. The freeing feeling of flying takes precedence over safety. He sees me and smiles. I say hi, always happy to see him and talk. He ducks his head and is polite, albeit never eager, in front of everyone else. In front of *them*, he acts macho and nonchalant, but in private he tells me things. He asks me what I think. He falls silent when I strike a nerve. He trusts me, and I want to take care of him. I smile and ask him when his bus is leaving. He tells me to board now, and we will talk later. If I get on the bus and bury myself in this memory so I can make him more real, my heart may truly break into pieces. But I see the bus, and I see him, and it seems I have no choice. I must go.

El sólo quiso jugar; El sólo quiso soñar; El sólo quiso amar pero el mundo lo olvidó[13]

He is sixteen again, and I am twenty-four. We are young and foolish to think our lives will follow the path we have planned for ourselves. But we don't care today as we get on the bus and travel the thirty minutes it takes to get into the capital. He doesn't collect bus fare from me, which irritates some of the people on the bus who don't know I take coffee to all the bus drivers on the 21 route … and have thus been awarded free passage on this bus line. Gato laughs at the people and winks at me. He knows I always get embarrassed about people thinking poorly of me. It is, after all, *I* who am the foreigner in *his* country. I don't want to stand out too much. Gato thinks this is funny when I try to explain it to him. He asks me how I think I *won't* stand out. He says it would help if I shrunk a foot and wore better shoes. Women don't wear such ugly shoes in his country, he tells me when my feet are stretched out comfortably in my Doc Marten sandals. He just shakes his head at me.

I feel the need to turn Juanes off and come back to reality. I am being swallowed up in this memory, and I am scared by what I feel. But I can't seem to make myself do it. I want to stay with Gato right now. I want to go around the curve between Santo Tomas and San Marcos and smell the burning garbage and see the lights of the town shining brightly across the mountain. I want to stay with him for a while. I want to stay warm. I don't want to go.

He looks at me, smiles, and asks me where I am headed. I tell him I am just going to Mejicanos to visit the MS boys and will be coming back before dark. I ask him when he will be done with work. He shrugs his shoulders and says he will be done when the last trip is taken for the day. I raise an eyebrow at him, and he sees I am not amused by his coyness. He laughs and tells me he will whistle when he sees me, and I know I will know it is him. We say goodbye until then.

> *El sólo quiso volar. El sólo quiso cantar. El sólo quiso amar, pero el mundo lo olvidó.*[14]

Chapter 2

It was morning, and the sun was already hard at work overheating the tin roofs of the shacks in San Salvador. The roosters hadn't stopped announcing the sunrise for a couple of hours, and they wouldn't until nighttime. Their internal clocks must have been off. People busied themselves getting ready for work and calling their children to wake up from their dreams and get dressed for school. Ladies in their mismatched skirts and too-tight Lycra tops sold pupusas[15] and other typical breakfasts to the bus drivers and vendors who had started work earlier that morning. Single men, in need of more than a Coke and sweet bread, ordered their plates of scrambled eggs, tortillas, and beans, and sat over their food, hurriedly chewing and swallowing so they could be on their way. Of course, there was always time to tell the cook she was beautiful and her food fabulous. When would she leave this job and come be their wife?

Sara was up already because her stomach had been hurting all night. She knew it wasn't something she had eaten. She realized that today would change her life forever, and she was tired before it began. She was fifteen, and the baby was not welcome. Part of her was excited because she had felt him move inside her. She watched her teenaged stomach move and take different shapes as he kicked and punched. People smiled at her and called her señora even though she wasn't married. She thought the baby could love her unconditionally. She had never had that, and she hoped the baby would complete her and fill her with joy, but she wasn't so sure that was possible.

But as she looked around the lean-to shack that was her home, the dirt floor on which she stood, the outhouse in which she relieved herself, she was smart enough to know what a baby meant for her future. It meant she would never be wanted by another man. After all, *a woman with kids isn't worth twenty-five cents.* She knew it meant she was finished before she had started. Her life was a cliché and a statistic. She knew she would have to work hard to feed and clothe her child. She knew it was the end to her education, even though she had already quit school years before … but now the dream of returning was dead as well. She knew the baby was the beginning of the end. She knew all those things, but she was in labor, so she called her mom.

On May 21, Wilfredo Antonio joined his mother in her poverty and despair. Little did he know, his constant companions would be injustice and emptiness; his siblings, rejection and pain; his playmates, anger and violence. But how could he know that now? So he drank his mother's milk and grew.

Sara worked as many jobs as she could find to pay the bills. She washed clothes and made pupusas to sell. As she bent over to scrub the stains out of others' clothes and rubbed her knuckles raw in the concrete washbasin, she imagined herself as a princess, locked up in a high tower, forced to do humiliating tasks. She would be rescued one day. She knew it in her heart.

As her eyes watered from the overpowering odor of the bleach, she looked at her sister, Norma, and couldn't imagine her fairytale fantasies anymore. She became angry and jealous instead. She didn't understand why Norma had a man who was sticking around. She didn't understand why Norma's son had a dad he could count on for a little extra money and companionship. Why was *she* the sister who had a bastard son? Why was *she* to be humiliated by the stares and gossip? Why should *she* be alone? She didn't understand, but what else could she do but continue working?

She and Norma began to make pupusas together. There were always people eager to pay for the tasty snack. As she carried the corn over to the miller to be ground, Wilfredo toddled after her. When she wrapped the corn meal around the bean and cheese filling, Wil opened his mouth so she would remember to drop a little cheese into it. He was cute, and he made her feel loved and accepted. Her own parents hadn't done that for her. They had always liked Norma better than her. Sara had been the one who received the ugly shoes that were on sale when Norma got to choose nicer ones. She had been the one asked to leave school first to help support the family. She had been the one given fewer beans out of the pot for dinner. She had been the second best.

So whenever Wil curled up to her chest and whispered, "I love you, Mommy," she felt peace. She kissed him and told him life wouldn't always be so bad. She promised to find him a father, and she swore to him he'd be able to have the same things as his cousins. He would never be second best.

Wil grew and was content in the life he had inherited. He played in the street with his cousins while their moms worked. He liked any type of game or toy, though he had no toys of his own per se. He played with whatever was available—a rock, a stick, a torn-up soccer ball. It didn't matter really. What did matter was that he could laugh and run free. Adults passing by to take the bus to work smiled at the barefoot boys as they giggled and played. They knew the boys would have responsibilities soon enough. It was good for kids to play, so they smiled and waved at them.

Wilfredo joked with his aunt Norma, telling her he was going to eat her up because she smelled like his favorite food—that always being on the days she fried pork rinds to sell to hungry passersby. He saw people who had things he didn't have, but when he went to sleep next to his mother at night, he was happy with her promises. He could even forget the times she hit him and screamed. He chose not to think of those times. He'd rather believe the lies she whispered in his ear at night.

And then one of the promises came true: she found another man. He lived in town and shouted cat-calls at her as she walked to the store to buy cheese, oil, or soap for one of her businesses. She was young, and she found the attention exhilarating. She hoped the cultural norm of her not being valuable anymore because of her child would no longer be true. She turned and smiled at Ernesto. He smiled back, and then he approached her.

It was a typical courtship. They ordered pupusas and laughed as they ate together. He came by her work and complimented her cooking loudly and boldly, embarrassing her a little, but not really. As they sipped their Cokes at a makeshift picnic table in a neighboring shack, he whispered how beautiful she was. As they walked down the road together, he reached out to take her hand. She always pushed him away out of obligation to her reputation. She had to pretend she didn't want to kiss him, and he had to play with her, pushing her to the point where she gave in, a little at a time. He promised her his love and honor. He vowed to care for her son as if he were his own. He promised to take care of her and never let another person say anything negative about her. He promised that he would be her protector, and she would be his woman. She would take care of him, and he would take care of her. And to the mind of a tired, twenty-year-old single mother, it sounded beautiful. So when he pushed her enough, Ernesto came to live with her, her son, her sister, and her nephews in their little shack.

Wil hoped his stepfather would be someone to play with and love. He hoped Ernesto would become his dad, but his hope was never realized. Ernesto grabbed it as a mere half-thought and twisted and distorted it to the point that Wil never fully recovered.

One of the things Sara had allowed herself to ignore during their courtship was Ernesto's penchant for alcohol. He drank too much and too often. He hit her and Wil. When he apologized to her, he said Wil had been a bother all day, and he had lost his temper. He just couldn't seem to understand that kid. He didn't think he was "right." He didn't think Wil allowed the love between Sara and him to work. Wil was sabotaging the relationship, and Ernesto didn't know how much he could handle.

Sara responded out of desperation. If Wil took too long to complete a task, she threw a bucket or spatula at his head. If he got underfoot while she prepared Ernesto's meal, she slapped him and sent him to bed without dinner. If he talked to her when she was attending to one of Ernesto's whims, he was thrown to the ground and kicked. Ernesto praised her for her disciplinary techniques. The boy had to learn, after all. In that way, Sara earned Ernesto's love, and Wil learned he could no longer ignore the pain. His mother's promises were lies. He learned to hate.

Ernesto continued to drink, and his yelling and screaming escalated. His demands on Sara's time multiplied, and Wil was left to fend for himself. His aunt helped him wash his clothes and fed him from the food she prepared for her own boys. Wil complained to his aunt about his life. He didn't understand his mom. His aunt said she didn't either. But there wasn't much love between the sisters, so she said too much sometimes. When Wil learned his mother didn't love him, and the words had come from the lips of his beloved aunt, he knew it must be true. When she told him his mom had never wanted him, he believed it.

He took all the pain and pressed it close to his heart. The imprint of it remained fresh forever.

Sara was miserable, but she believed it was the best life she could have. She had to keep hold of Ernesto. She couldn't stand the thought of life without him because she needed him. She had to have the protection of a man. And what was a woman without a man to care for? She had been raised in a culture that wouldn't give her much thought without a man by her side. She had to keep him, so she did whatever she needed to do. She waited up for him when he came home drunk and pleasured him as he saw fit. She woke up at late hours to make him dinner he had missed, even though in a few short hours she would have to begin her day of work. She washed his clothes, met his every need and desire, and gave him all her money to spend on whatever he chose. And, of course, she forsook her son to prove her loyalty to Ernesto and her willingness to do whatever it took to keep his love. How could Ernesto not love her?

Of course, she yelled and got mad at her husband sometimes. How could she not? He drank away her hard-earned money and caused her more trouble. She told him he should leave her a little money to feed Wil. After all, Wil's cries gave her a headache. She threw in Ernesto's face all the empty promises he had made to her. She got mad, but when he yelled back and she felt she might lose him, she gave in and did whatever she could to make peace. And so, she got pregnant.

Ernesto was overjoyed at the prospect of having

his own child. He wanted his own blood in the family and not some bastard child of another man. He hated Wil for what he represented—that another man had been with his woman. He blamed young Wil. He told Wil that once the baby was born, he'd be gone from the house. He told Wil he was nothing, and that his mom would do whatever Ernesto told her to do. Wil had no voice. Wil had no rights. Wil was someone who could be disposed of without anyone caring. And seven-year-old Wil knew it was true.

Sara took care of herself during the nine months of her pregnancy. She didn't want anything to happen to her new baby. He had to be healthy. He had to be smart. He must have the very best because he was her security. She knew Ernesto wouldn't leave her if she had his son. She was happy, and Wil was scared. He didn't know what to expect, but he hoped his mom would love him more once she had a second baby. He would be a helpful son and a great big brother. He would show her she needed him, and he would do his best to earn her love.

But just as Wil had been born to share his mother's poverty and despair and live in constant rejection, Armando was born knowing he was the favored son. When he took his first sip of his mother's milk, he became poisoned against Wil. He knew if he said Wil had done something, Wil would be hit. He knew if he wanted something, he only had to ask. He knew if he wanted something of Wil's, he could take it, and Wil would be beaten for demanding it back.

Armando's clothes were always clean and ironed,

laid out with loving care by his mother while Wil had to wash his own. Armando was given the meat that cooked with the beans while Wil got only beans. Armando was stronger and healthier. He was taller and better-looking. He was the good son and deserved to be treated well. Wil was just trash, an unfortunate reality. Ernesto and Sara gave him food, a place to live, and clothes to wear; what else should be expected of them? They did what they could for an ungrateful waste of life. And Wil breathed in the poison that consumed everyone else and began to hate himself.

When he was nine, Wil received a rabbit. He fell in love with the little white fluffy creature for much the same reason his mom had felt some excitement about him when she had been pregnant. He reasoned that the rabbit might be able to give him the unconditional love he sought. He fed the bunny, brushed it, played with it, carried it around, and talked to it for hours at a time. It became his life. He had his cousins and his aunt, but they were busy with their own lives. They didn't always have time for him, but his rabbit did. His mom, brother, and Ernesto didn't want to be bothered with him, but his rabbit liked hearing him.

One day, Ernesto arrived home drunk and got angry because Sara had gone into San Salvador with Armando to buy some food. Ernesto wanted food, and since he was not accustomed to having to do anything for himself, he raged that his woman wasn't there. His breath reeked of cheap booze; his eyes were red and parched from the dust that constantly swirled around town and, together with his dirty clothes from having spent the night in the street where he had landed after his last shot of whiskey, Ernesto was a menacing presence. When Ernesto saw Wil, skinny and huddled in the corner with the rabbit, his anger boiled over. He was hungry and stuck at home with the bastard child he hated. He started screaming and wandering around the house.

Wil got nervous for his rabbit. He knew Ernesto was looking for something to beat him with, and he wanted to spare the rabbit's innocence. His had been stripped away long ago, so he went and put his rabbit away in a little box. Ernesto saw him trying to hide the rabbit, and Wil's fear for the rabbit convicted Ernesto of his abusive sins. But instead of choosing repentance, he grabbed a brick. Ernesto's eyes were crazed from too much alcohol and unbridled fury. Wil screamed before it even happened. Ernesto's hands came down and beat the rabbit to death as Wil watched, crying and screaming. He tried to throw himself between the brick and the bunny, but Ernesto kicked him out of the way. He passed out.

When he woke up, Wil's stomach hurt. He looked around and saw the blood-and-fur-covered box. He started to cry but stopped himself. He wouldn't give Ernesto the satisfaction. He picked up the box and went and dug a hole outside behind the house. He fell asleep on the earth covering his beloved pet. When his aunt came home from work, Wil told her what had happened. She hugged him and apologized. She told him his mom wouldn't do anything to help him, so he shouldn't bother telling her. His mother loved

Ernesto more than him, or hadn't he noticed? Wil nodded. He had noticed.

He was a sad boy who carried on living simply because there was nothing else to do. He went to school and studied as hard as he could. But sometimes, the pain from a beating or the ache in his empty stomach hindered his academic progress. When the school bell rang and school let out, Wil headed home shuffling his feet. He didn't want to rush to his destination. Nothing of value awaited him there. He noticed the gang members in the Ceiba[16] as he trudged home. They always seemed to be having fun. They wore their baggy clothes and flashed their signs. Everyone said they were delinquents and would kill anyone who got in their way. Still, Wil had noticed their smiles and cocky self-assuredness.

They said hi to him as he shuffled home in his dirty and badly-pressed school uniform. He barely acknowledged them for fear of what they might do to him. They sensed his vulnerability. They could see the scars on his arms. They noticed he wouldn't lift his head. They saw themselves in him and wanted to cure him of his fear and depression so they wouldn't have to remember their own despair. One or two began to walk alongside him as he traveled home. They asked him if he wanted a mango with chile and lemon or if he would like a Coke to cool his throat. They told him it was on them. They liked him and said he was cool. And Wil hungered for their words and devoured the food they offered.

One day when they were all sitting around him

while he drank a Coke, telling their stories and joking about which jaina[17] they were going to go out with that night, he told them about his rabbit and Ernesto. They burned with rage as they remembered their pain when something dear had been stripped from them. They told Wil they could help him. They promised to protect him. They welcomed him into their family. And Wil's head spun as he realized people *did* want him. He embraced them, and they punched and kicked him for the required thirteen seconds. Wil was born again, and his name became Gato.

Chapter 3

Gato was ten when he formally began plotting Ernesto's death. He wanted his stepfather to die so he could have a life with his mother. Naively, he thought his mom would love him again if Ernesto was gone. Little did he know, Ernesto's love was the necessary justification for her to take out her true feelings on him.

Gato came home one night with a new gang tattoo sketched on his arm. He hadn't had the guts to feel the needle yet. That would be a frightening experience for later when one gang member would hold him down, while another took a needle and ink pump to his body and began marking him for life. They would all be drunk, and the needle would leave stray marks and memories of pain and friendship intertwined. However, today, it was a mere sketch, but Ernesto saw it and yelled.

Sara grabbed Gato and started screaming. How could he dishonor them by hanging out with gang members? How could he be so ungrateful for all he had? And now he was hanging out with killers? They would show him. And as Sara held him down, Ernesto took his cigarette and burned holes along Gato's back.

"So you like to have your body all marked up? That's good…I'm going to help you, you little son of a bitch."

He screamed in pain and struggled to get free. Sara kicked him as he fell to the ground. She was encouraged by Ernesto's jeers. The little bastard wanted to live on the street. He wanted to kill the family. He was evil and a good-for-nothing. He needed to be taught a lesson. So they threw him out into the street to be raised by the gang members who told him they loved him.

When the police found Gato, his scrawny body was huddled in a corner of the Ceiba, starving and shivering. They saw he had been abused, but they didn't pay much attention to it. The country was in the middle of a civil war, poverty and violence were rampant, and survival was the order of the day. It was not the time to deal with domestic issues. They called his mom, and she couldn't be found. They called his aunt, and she came and got him. They told her he had stolen food from a vendor and that they could throw him into jail for that. She paid the money he owed and took him home.

As she undressed him to put his pajamas on, he sucked in his breath from the pain of the cloth pulling against his newly scabbed wounds, and she began to cry. His back was burned and bruised. His ribs were exposed. He just curled up against her, exhausted. He was happy to feel the warmth of someone else. He smelled her clothes and sighed deeply. She picked the lice from his hair. She washed his back and dressed his sores. She knew he would be hit again, but she gave him a moment of maternal concern. She laid him into the bed and went to make dinner for her sons.

When Ernesto and Sara saw Gato's battered body back in the house, their initial response was anger. Hadn't they told him he no longer lived there? What gave that boy the nerve to think he had any right to be in their house, let alone the bed? But Gato's aunt exaggerated the story with the police. She said they threatened to put Sara and Ernesto in jail for abuse if they found him on the streets again. Ernesto grabbed Sara's hand and pulled her aside. Perhaps they should let the boy stay there, at least until the danger of discovery passed. They wouldn't burn him again. They wouldn't make any more evidence. Then they could get rid of him. Sara agreed and made dinner for Ernesto and Armando. She didn't even go to kiss her son or look at him as he lay sleeping in bed. She could tell Ernesto was nervous. She would have to soothe him. But she had so much washing to do, where would she find the time?

Gato remained living at home, eating the leftovers, and receiving the tidbits of affection thrown his way from his aunt and mother. He also remained in the gang. His resentment grew stronger, and his desire for Ernesto's blood never abated. He would see him die; he *must* see him die. He just didn't know how he could do it without getting caught. He quit school to dedicate his time and energy to his new passion, the Mara Salvatrucha.[18]

Ernesto knew his stepson hated him, but he didn't care. Gato was no one to take seriously—a small child, angry perhaps, but a child. Ernesto ruled the house, and he wasn't about to let a kid tell him anything. He continued working when he wasn't drunk. He delivered bundles of goods to different stores. He was a deliveryman, and he was good at it. He knew how to talk to the clientele. He could make the women blush and the men laugh. He could be charming when he wanted to be. Only his family saw his brutish side. Only they were privy to his frightening rage and demanding spirit. So he worked and did well for himself.

Then one day, he was delivering his goods in the afternoon, when a bus driver lost control of his microbus and slammed into him, sending Ernesto flying through the air to land on the sidewalk, bloody and bruised. An older woman, one whom he had told was beautiful, screamed and called the ambulance. By the time it arrived, he was dead. And even though Ernesto's tyranny had ended with his last breath, his legacy continued to thrive.

When Sara heard the news, she fell to the dirt floor of her house and wept. Her small, exhausted body rocked back and forth in anguish. She had two boys and no man. She was only in her twenties. What would she do? She would die; her life was over as surely as Ernesto's. Armando toddled to his mother's side. She hugged him and cried. Armando cried too because his father had been good to him. Gato just walked out of the house and went to see his homeboys. No one noticed he was gone.

Gato's homeboys handed him a beer and congratulated him on his loss. Gato drank and celebrated the death of his stepfather. He yelled out all of Ernesto's trespasses and felt great relief that it was over. His homeboys punctuated Gato's statements with their own comments.

"The son of a bitch deserved it."

"That asshole is burning in hell like he should be."

"The world is better without him."

His homeboys were happy for their new recruit, but the more Gato drank, the more he realized his life might not get better. His mother's abuse had commingled with that of Ernesto's. She hated him too. It hadn't been *just* Ernesto. It had been both of them. And what about Armando? Why did his little brother hate him so much? He'd try to fix that. He'd bring him treats, and Armando would forget his dad and love Gato like a brother should.

Gato was eleven and, as expected, Sara didn't begin to love him. She blamed *him* for Ernesto's death, even though Gato had had nothing to do with it. Logic told her that, but she was so sad and confused, she didn't care. She wanted—no, needed—to blame someone for Ernesto's death. She wrapped up all her disappointments and hurts, her bad mistakes and decisions, and threw them in Gato's face. It was his fault, and he was to blame. Had he not been born, none of this would be her life. She would have had a good life with money and education and a man by her side. Gato was a sin, and she chose to hate him.

Chapter 4

"What's up, man? What have you been up to?" Gato entered the dirty hovel where Oso sat. He had to side-step the broken glass, drying lugeys, and puddles of urine that gave the place its unique smell. It was a "destroyer," duly named for its caved-in roof, broken windows, and lack of doors. No one had lived in the abandoned shack that sat at the end of an overgrown path outside of town for some time, so the gang members had moved in and made it their clubhouse. They shook hands with the requisite gang signal accompaniment. Oso passed a joint to Gato, who inhaled deeply.

"Everything's cool, man. I've just been hanging around, nothing more. And you, where have you been?"

Gato gave Oso back the joint and relaxed against the wall of the destroyer. "Around here, you know how it is."

A few other gang members from the Mara Salvatrucha entered the little room and took their hits on the joint, shaking hands with everyone who was gathering. One of them wasn't paying attention and stepped in the puddle of pee. "Sonofa..." His words ran together as the other gang members burst out laughing at their friend's folly. Oso cleared his throat, and the boys gathered around him like students do with their teacher. Oso was the designated leader of the Santo Tomas clique. He was young, but totally covered with tattoos, having fully dedicated himself to the gang. The other boys looked up to him, including Gato, who was his best friend.

"You all know we are here because we have some things to get done. Our clique needs to grow and be more powerful. First of all, we need more women."

The guys all chuckled, and their comments became rank. Oso continued, "We also need money. We'll start by asking people for a coin here or there—nothing major. If we need to, we can rob some people downtown ... but never here in the neighborhood. We have to respect where we come from, and we don't need enemies here."

"Yeah," they all agreed, while some lit cigarettes and opened their bottles of liquor.

"Gato, you are in charge of the new members. You have a good relationship with the kids at the school, so go and find us some other crazy guys for the gang."

Gato nodded his head; he liked the idea of that assignment. He started thinking of the boys he had gone to school with. There was Antonio. He was big and handsome. He would be good protection for the gang, and he would bring women into the clique. Antonio liked to fight, so he was a good choice. There was Jaime. He always looked in the direction of the gang members when they were enjoying themselves in the Ceiba. He might be interested in joining up. Gato took a drag of his cigarette and kept thinking.

"Now, homies, it is time to have some fun. We

are going to the dance tonight and look for some sexy girls. It is going to be great. I am going to find me a nice chubby one like I like."

The boys laughed and continued drinking and smoking, working on their highs before the dance started. They wanted to be at ease when talking to the pretty girls who were bound to be there. It was easy to get the girls' attention; there weren't a lot of tattooed bad boys roaming around the town at that time. They were different, and different was interesting. When they all got up and steadied themselves on unsure, tipsy legs, they headed out to the dance.

They made it without incident to the soccer field, which the townspeople had converted into a dance floor and small stage for the local band that would be the night's entertainment. Gato walked around with the boys, looking at all the people gathered to forget their problems and have a little fun. There was very little modesty in the young girls' attire at these affairs. All the boys couldn't help but gawk when an attractive girl walked by in a sequined bra and mini skirt. They shoved each other and laughed, saying they would help her take the bra off later that night. Gato laughed and enjoyed the show, but he didn't see who he was looking for, so he walked over to the main gate of the field and smoked a cigarette. Another gang member, Loco, joined Gato at the gate.

"Gato, do you see someone you like?"

"No, man, I'm waiting for someone in particular. She hasn't shown up yet, but she's the best girl in town."

"What if she doesn't show?"

Gato just shrugged his shoulders. She'd told him she'd be there. He was desperate to see her. To him, she was the most beautiful girl he had ever seen. He had always known her, since they had grown up in the same town. Now, however, when she talked to him, he felt warm and happy. He wanted to feel that forever, so she *had* to come to the dance.

"Do you have something I can drink, or did we leave it in the destroyer?"

"Of course. Here you go."

Loco handed Gato the bottle of liquor, then got distracted by a passing girl wearing very tight pants and a low-cut shirt. He followed her and grabbed her hand. Gato chuckled to himself. He took a drink and waited some more. She had to come to the dance.

And then she appeared—a picture of youth and innocence in her yellow shirt and short denim skirt. Her black shoes clashed, but they were the only heels she had, and it was a dance after all, so she had to have heels.

Gato had been leaning against the wall, but when he saw her, he stood upright, excited, not very gangster-like at all. He couldn't hide his joy at seeing her, and as he approached her, Ana's cheeks grew warm and flushed.

"Hi, gorgeous, how are you? You look more than beautiful, my love," Gato wooed her.

Ana smiled and looked down. She knew he liked her, and she couldn't help but feel something for him as well. He was special, even if he was a gang member, a throwaway kid. Something was different about him.

"Thanks, Gatito. You look good yourself. Were you waiting a long time? I hope not. My mom didn't want to let me come, but my brother came to protect me … so." She rolled her eyes, and Gato acknowledged Juan by going over and shaking hands with him and making small talk.

"I'll take good care of her, I promise."

"Well, you have to, and if you disrespect her in any way, you will pay for it," Juan threatened.

Gato chuckled and said he understood and that he would never disrespect Ana. She was worth too much for that.

"Remember what I said, man. And you two better not disappear anywhere either. I have to know where she is at all times."

"Don't worry, man. I will take good care of her, and we will be right here the whole time," Gato assured him.

Juan left the two of them alone, but not before shooting Ana a warning glance, the type big brothers give to their little sisters to tell them they will have major problems if they don't behave … and not just from their parents. Ana smiled at her brother and told him to go have fun. Gato had, of course, put his cigarette out and hidden the bottle when he had first seen Ana. He had now forgotten about it completely as he grabbed her by the hand and led her to the dance floor.

They danced to the music even though the melody often got lost as it passed through the lower-quality speakers at full volume. Nobody really cared that the music was being swallowed up by feedback and static or that the problem could be lessened by turning down the amplifiers even a little. The beauty of the music was found in its earsplitting decibel level.

Gato held Ana close on some of the slower songs, and she relaxed her body into his. Gato smelled her hair, the scent of tortillas being cooked over open fire and floral shampoo. He smiled and felt happy. He didn't know why she was so different from every other girl he had seen and known, but she was. He felt safe when he was with her, at peace with himself when he saw himself in her eyes. Ana looked up at Gato at the close of the song, and even though the music to the next song was running over the top of it, she didn't hear anything but her breath and his. "I love you," she whispered. And he bent down and kissed her softly, tenderly, and joyously.

Chapter 5

Gato and Ana were in love. They were young to be sure, and thirteen-year-olds shouldn't be making adult decisions. But in a culture where children worry about their next meal and see violence of the worst kind, both in their homes and on the street, where soap operas and their twisted dramas, along with vicious action movies, are watched by toddlers resting on their mothers' laps, teenagers are considered adults by most standards.

So Gato and Ana spent time together talking, kissing, laughing, and getting mad at each other. Gato tested out his burgeoning macho behavior on her. She responded, at first, by being flattered by his jealousies and demands, but then it began to wear on her.

"So do you want to be with the guy I caught you talking with? I saw you! You are a horrible woman. I bet you don't even love me now, right?" he accused her.

She reassured him that she only wanted him, and deep down he knew that, but he thought holding onto the suspicions and jealousy made him more of a man. And she put up with it because that was what women did in their culture—the true proof of love, right?

She showed up at his house and washed his clothes for him as any good girlfriend would. He watched her bent over the concrete washbasin cleaning his clothes, her black wavy hair falling out of the loose ponytail, and felt very strongly that he needed to hug her and never let her go. But he couldn't do that; the emotion was too strong for a man to show. So instead, he complimented her work on the bleached white shirts, kissed her on the cheek, and then ate pupusas with her that he begged off his mom and aunt. She wiped her sweating brow with the back of her hand, pushed her hair back off her face, and then opened his pupusas to stuff with cabbage relish before she ate her own.

Sometimes she felt like his mom, and she caught him looking at her oddly … unlike other men had looked at her, but she never analyzed it carefully. She knew Gato's mom hadn't been the best caretaker. Maybe Gato, when he looked at her with that mixture of hurt and delight, was thinking about other things. She just knew she wanted to help him and show him she loved him. She didn't understand why he didn't always reciprocate.

It saddened her when he stood her up for his homeboys. She didn't know how many times she waited for him to come see her, and he didn't. She'd get mad. "I'm not always going to be here putting up with all of this crap. If you want to be with me, prove it to me. You have to choose between your homeboys and me," she told him.

His reaction was always swift and repentant. He needed to get her calm so he wouldn't have to make that fateful decision. He couldn't leave the gang, the one family he had, but how could he live without her? So he kissed her and assured her she was his life.

"Oh baby, how could you even think I don't love you? You are my world, my life, and my heart. I dream about you and want to spend my whole life with you. You are the only one who understands me. I love you. Don't make me choose. The guys think you are great, too. They are my family; how could you ask me to choose? You have to undersand me, my love," he pleaded with her. And she tried to understand him as best she could, so no choice was made.

When they had sex for the first time, she was nervous, and he was eager. Gato had been asking for it for over a year, so she felt she should show him how she felt. It didn't last long, but when he held her close to him afterward, she felt happy and warm by his side. Now she was his woman *officially*. They were not quite fifteen.

When her family found out, because news travels fast in a small town where anyone's most private moments are everyone else's news, she received a firm slap on the face and a harsh ultimatum. "You dirty whore, how could you give yourself away so easily and to such a lowlife? He is trash, a stinking gangster with nothing to show for himself. That's it... there will be no more of this, or you will no longer be a part of this family."

She cried and yelled that they didn't understand. She loved him, and he loved her. But they only saw a stupid girl who had been drawn into a gangster's lies and would be ruined if they didn't do something quickly. She refused to stop seeing him, so they called a family member who lived in a different state.

"You are going to go live with your uncle up north. And if we find out you have communicated with Gato, or if he finds you, we will give your uncle permission to kill him," they told her with finality.

They packed a bag of her belongings, and as she was pushed on the bus the next morning by her mother and brother who accompanied her, a tear fell from her eye and down her cheek. She never saw Gato again.

When Gato went to see her and found out she was gone, and no one would tell him where his Ana had gone, he found comfort in his bottle of liquor down at the Ceiba. His homeboys gathered around him and offered him their half-smoked cigarettes and words of condolence. When night fell and darkness made everything look like he was feeling, he wept.

Chapter 6

Flashing gang signs in his baggy clothes, Gato felt like a king in the Ceiba. He stood on the cracking cement steps leading up to the cathedral that so many saints and those seeking repentance had climbed for years. He asked for money. Some gave it to him without a second thought, while others brushed past him, either ignoring him or cursing him under their breath ... after all, it was just one more sin to confess to the patient priest who might be asleep in the warm and cozy confessional after hearing so many sins. He cat-called the reverent girls with their heads bowed in modesty at the sides of their protective mothers. He laughed when their moms turned to glare at him yelling, "Punk!" He shouted insults at humble men on their way to work in someone else's fields for a pittance of pay. They didn't even look his way, as if his verbal insults commingled with their own mental batterings of themselves. The Ceiba was MS[19] territory, and he was one of the leaders of the clique, having spent six years of his not-so-innocent childhood with them.

No one was going to hurt him again. He was a man now. At sixteen, he made his own money working for the 21 bus line. He was a cobrador, collecting money from the passengers and enjoying his rides back and forth between home and downtown. It didn't hurt that he could flirt with all the pretty girls who rode the bus. He thought himself to be quite the catch ... a little dangerous, a little kind, a little tough, a little affectionate, a little of everything, dressed in highly starched and pressed gang wear. He was proud, and his palpable arrogance made people look at him.

When he was at work, he joked with the other bus drivers—a motley crew of men not much more respected than gang members themselves. They cursed and spit and made lewd jokes *about* women, *to* women, *around* women ... it didn't matter which preposition preceded women; the crass humor remained. They punched each other and laughed at each other's expense.

"Hey, asshole, you look horrible, man. Son of a bitch, you scared me."

"Shut up, fag. You aren't good at anything; that's why your woman is out looking for it in other places."

"Sonofa ... I'm gonna kill you."

Laughter ensued as the other bus drivers egged on the arguments or punctuated them with other insults. On and on it went for hours, day in and day out, a brotherhood of mostly uneducated, disorderly, womanizing misfits who hadn't had either the luck or the ambition to get a better job than what they had at the bus line.

The guys on the 21 route had different nicknames. In fact, very few of them could identify each other by their real names. It was nicknames that stamped one as being part of the group.

Some of the nicknames were basic and related to

physical features: "Negro" was given to someone who was dark-skinned; "Chele" for someone with light skin; "Gringo" if one could speak English; "Gato" if one's eyes were lighter and shaped like a cat's; "Panzon" if one had a belly; "Flaco" if one was too skinny; "Pelon" was given to someone who had shaved his head and had no hair; the one called "Gusano" had a worm-like scar crawling down his stomach from a childhood surgery.

Some nicknames were received based on actions: "Raro" was weird in both actions and speech; "Diablo[20]" received his dubious name because of his reputation as a bad boy; "Gata" got his nickname for hanging out too much with Gato, so he was teased for being his wife.

Perhaps the worst nicknames were those based on appearance. Seldom flattering, they made one laugh when thinking about the meaning. For instance, "Cuche Ruso" didn't look like a Russian pig, but the active imaginations of the bus drivers must have envisioned him as one because the name stuck. "Pie Grande[21]" was also called "Comeniños[22]" because of his severe demeanor. "Vampirata" and "Chupacabra[23]" looked like the mythical creatures they were named after. "Chorizo" apparently looked like sausage to someone. "Panda Oso[24]" was chubby with white skin and black hair. "Garobo" had hair that stood on end and a smushed face, making him appear like a giant lizard. "Pinocho" had a big nose, thus labeling him forever as the little wooden boy.

Other nicknames must have been leftovers thrust

upon an unsuspecting victim. "Rosa Salvage" didn't look like a wild rose at all. "Caballo Rojo" wasn't red or horse-like. "Semasforo" was named for a stoplight; did he run them? Perhaps.

To be surrounded by friends with whom he could laugh and joke was a warm place to be, and Gato savored his time with them. It was hard work with long hours, sometimes reaching fourteen hours a day, but it was worth it. Gato got along with them and felt a part of the group of men. They teased him and shoved his head or grabbed it and rubbed their knuckles into his scalp like any big brother would. They chastised him for sweet-talking a female customer too long and then having to rush to collect the bus fare from everyone else. They whispered encouragement to him when he got close enough to smell a girl's hair and steal a kiss from her.

Most of his time was spent with these men, but his spare time was dedicated to the gang. They were his blood brothers, his supporters in the worst of times, his fellow drinkers and carousers, his friends, and his life.

Chapter 7

As I packed my bags, deciding what to take and what to leave behind, I looked out the window and saw the typical rainfall that made Washington State both infamous and beautiful. I would leave there that night, not to return for the next two years. My destination was San Salvador and, my dream about to be realized, I sorted through my clothes.

My mom and younger sisters stood in the door-way watching me, laughing at me, and just talking. I would miss them very much as it turned out, but I wasn't thinking about them in that moment; my focus was on that flight to Central America. Having studied El Salvador's politics, I couldn't wait to go and see the places I read about, cried over, only felt tacitly, but needed to feel tangibly. I had been planning this all my life, even though I didn't know El Salvador would be my destination until two years earlier. I had always pictured myself in South Africa, fighting with the African National Congress[25] and championing equal rights for all. When I heard Ladysmith Black Mambazo, an acoustic musical group from South Africa, in concert, and talked with the singers after the show, I think I shocked them with the fact that I knew what was happening in their country.

But something in college shifted my attention away from Africa and onto Central America. Perhaps it was the fact that Nelson Mandela was out of prison and then President DeKlerk had called for the official end to apartheid. Things seemed to be on the mend there. Perhaps it was all the friends I had made my freshman year of college who were from Central America. Some would probably say it was the fabulous Dr. Ricardo Sanchez, who taught me more than Chicano literature at Washington State University that semester. He had told me to get over myself and my sadness, to shake off the hurt and pain I held close to my heart after the deaths of my father, my friend, and my best friend and begin to live, to learn Spanish, to breathe it and then allow myself to flow as was intended into every crevice that existed.

It could have been in my genes; my dad read endless books on Latin America for his own enjoyment, and my mother told my three sisters and me that we had been born with a purpose and that our lives were not just about us, but that we must serve God in whatever capacity we could. Maybe it was Dr. Rachel May from the University of Washington in Tacoma, who only had to open her mouth, and the years of rich, tactile history of Latin America, the bloodshed and glory, the exciting and the mundane, the brutal and the beautiful would come alive in my mind and draw me into the panoramic. She was a tough grader, and she pushed and stretched me to become more than a student, to be a thinker, an analyzer of words and actions. Perhaps it was a little need to prove those wrong who told me I would not make it to another country, and if I made it, I would not last there. Or maybe it was

God, weaving their inspiration, encouragement, criticism, teaching, examples, and wisdom into one complete blanket of reason to focus my energy, ability, time, and talents and go forth.

Whatever it was, my mind was fixated on El Salvador and had been for two years, since the day I had sat with a map outstretched in front of me pointing to different countries and saying their names aloud. "Chile, Chile, Chile … no … Argentina, Argentina, Argentina … no … Cuba, Cuba, Cuba … no … Nicaragua, Nicaragua, Nicaragua … no … El Salvador, El Salvador, El Salvador"—strange peace, and then—"El Salvador, El Salvador, yes." My studies shifted to El Salvador. If Rachel May taught on the church in Latin America, then I wrote on the church in El Salvador. If she taught about grassroots movements, I focused on those in El Salvador. If we were to analyze a current political situation in Latin America and make our predictions for the future, I wrote on the FMLN and their potential victories and downfalls. El Salvador became my love. And so I had to go.

My mom took me to the airport that night and kissed me goodbye. I couldn't cry, even though she and my sisters were. The transportation to my dream was there in the doorframe of the plane. I waved goodbye and yelled out rather flippantly, though innocently, "I'll see you in two years," a huge smile on my face, and then I was off.

I couldn't sleep on the plane, even though my flight left Seattle at midnight. My stomach was in knots, and I was overly eager to see the land I had loved with such passion, even without knowing it. I hadn't learned Spanish as Dr. Sanchez had advised. I had studied some vocabulary. I'd be able to spew forth a list of words like *abrelatas, cuna, cortinas, vaca, pizarra, bandera, silla, cama, bistec, finca, escritorio, baño, disco compacto,* and so forth.[26] It would be interesting communicating with the people, but I felt very prepared in spite of that. In retrospect, I was very naïve.

I was to be a missionary teaching English in a private elementary school. Today, there are not many missionaries called merely to preach. One has to be able to serve in some other capacity, which was fine for me, because I didn't think I should be preaching to anyone. I had never liked people preaching to me anyway. And while I had never been a teacher, I had worked as a teacher's aide for a couple of years while studying for my BA. I loved teenagers with lots of behavior problems. I liked the challenge, the attitude they threw my way. So I felt ready to take on the challenge. Had I been able to see myself in the next couple of months, struggling to maintain calm in the classroom and becoming overly agitated with the students, I think I may have gone home right then. But, luckily, life does not always present itself openly and honestly. The hard, and sometimes most rewarding, part is the slow unwrapping of life's surprises and disappointments.

When I landed, I hadn't slept for over twenty-four hours. I wasn't tired so much as shell-shocked. The airport was under construction, and people forced their way through the lines and immigration, and a true war was being waged at baggage claim. I waited, hoping the people from my flight would grab their things and move on, so I could make my way to the baggage carousel and take possession of mine. But I was only swarmed and jostled again by the next group of people from another flight. It was a nightmare. I couldn't breathe because the heat and humidity were overwhelming to someone who had lived in western Washington for the last five years, and I couldn't understand a word people were saying. "Can opener" and "farm" are stupid words in situations like that. I realized I had entered my dream, and my dream was shoving me to the back of the line.

To this day, I do not know how Carlos, the young man sent to pick me up from the airport, found me, drenched in sweat and overcome with frustration in the corner of the baggage claim, with shoes full of footprints and unshed tears, but he did. He shoved his way to the front, pulling me along for the ride, using the right amount of politeness and forcefulness, a skill I have yet to master in the Spanish or even English language, for that matter. He asked if I was okay, the look of shock and horror having fully registered on my face. I told him I would be fine if we could leave. He laughed, grabbed my bags, and pulled me through the next crowd of people to the airport exit.

Carlos was a young man from a wealthy family in San Salvador, who had taken a job with the school, only to perfect his English. He did this by escorting the American missionaries who came to El Salvador to work. Because he spoke English, it gave me the wonderful opportunity to question him about the politics of the region. He laughed at me. "You aren't like the other missionaries who come here. Why do you know about the FMLN and ARENA?[27] Why do you care? Are you a Communist?"

We laughed and talked on the hour-and-a-half trip to my new home. I fell silent at times, then blurted out comments when we'd pass certain areas of the countryside. "I didn't know it would be so magical, so incredibly breathtaking here. It is marvelous. The green is like what green was meant to be when someone chose the name for it. The colors are so vibrant and spellbinding. How does it feel to live here?"

Carlos looked at me and shook his head. "You have read too many books and watched too many movies. This is a poor country … look and smell … it stinks here. And all that color you like, it will turn brown in the dry season."

"You are such a happy person, Carlos … wow. Why are you such a pessimist?"

"You will see that my country is made up of poor, stupid people, who don't know how to take care of themselves. Everything stinks and makes me want to throw up. That man with the cow that we saw back there on the road, that you thought was so cool, it's an embarrassment. This country needs to change, and the people need to change or else El Salvador will always be the worst type of place," he said disdainfully.

"You're a snob," I countered, half-seriously and half-jokingly, trying to lighten the souring mood.

"I'm a realist, and you're a Communist, romantic

fool. Just wait until you have to talk to the people and deal with them. They will cheat you and laugh at you and call you a stupid gringa. So you may sympathize with my people and their poverty and all that they have suffered, or you can grow up and get smarter. No one here will change." He rolled his eyes at me and then faced forward as we drove through the small, crowded streets.

We drove the rest of the way with Carlos pointing out all the stupidity of his country, rolling down the windows when we passed certain places, making me smell the burning rubber and the raw meat that someone was selling spoiling in the sun. "How beautiful, right?" he asked sarcastically. Yet, I did think it was beautiful. I was enchanted by El Salvador. Carlos's ideas and thoughts, and even his real knowledge of the place, couldn't change that.

Unfortunately, my first few months in El Salvador weren't quite the fairytale I had imagined they would be; they were more like the horrible picture Carlos had painted that first day. I had no control in my classroom, having not figured out the balance between being a friend and a teacher. I got sick with a kidney infection, high blood pressure, and an assortment of other ailments that I'd never had before and haven't had since. This prompted a week-long hospital stay in San Salvador, where only a blood transfusion got me back on my feet.

Carlos didn't help, telling me I would die of dengue, a disease like malaria that would ravage my body and destroy me. In disgust, he covered his mouth and nose with a handkerchief and left, running for his car. That was the last I saw of him. I was bored, because I didn't have a way to get places and had been told I would be raped and killed if I rode in the buses that were the primary mode of transportation in El Salvador. I wanted to get out and explore. I wanted to touch, eat, breathe, experience, and *live* El Salvador. And then, I got my chance.

Our school facility was being purchased, and the actual school being consolidated with another near the capital. I would be moving, and I would have more freedom. I was very excited at the prospect, although I had managed to make one friend out where I was and was very sad about leaving her. I said goodbye to her, and she refused to hug me. She said all gringos were the same. They used people and were then off to exploit the next group. I was one of them, so I should just go. I tried to hug her anyway, understanding why she was angry. America's history in the region hadn't been positive due to our intervention during El Salvador's civil war. The "ugly American" stereotype had never been fully eliminated. I was sad to be associated with it, but I said goodbye.

I closed my eyes and silently remembered my few months in that town. I visualized the time when another missionary and I had driven too fast down the beach road in the pouring rain to outrace the canopy of lightning. Its bright, almost blinding iridescence, halted all conversation; We had known we were in the presence of God Almighty, the only one who could control it and send it crashing to the ground.

I remembered waking up at sunrise to milk the cows I never could get milked, and hearing little voices laughing at me, correcting me, and small hands showing me the right way.

I saw the fat toad in the corner of my shower and the cockroaches crawling along my shower walls, and heard my pleading and bargaining with them to stay where they were, while promising in return that I would stay where I was. I would miss that first haunt of mine in El Salvador for all of its moments—good *and* bad.

I got in the car and headed to my new destination.

Chapter 8

I loved my new town. It was much closer to the capital, and I didn't feel so isolated. As we pulled up, we passed a row of shacks where women were selling pupusas and tortillas. Young men who had discarded their shirts were changing flat tires and joining the bus drivers in watching the passing women and joking with each other about life and conquests. A group of older men were eating at Comedor "Tita,"[28] watching a small television mounted in the corner of the outdoor dining area. They grunted as the news reporter rambled on, telling them of the government's new promises and the arguments that had ensued in the legislative assembly between the rival political parties.

My new home was bigger and nicer. I didn't have to share my bathroom with toads or possums like before, although the occasional cockroach made its appearance and sent me right back into early-morning negotiations, while my body was pressed tightly into a corner of the shower. I also got the hang of the classroom. I learned the delicate balance of being friendly, but not a friend; maintaining the professional distance, while still being able to laugh at a good joke or hug a crying child.

My Spanish was improving as well. My vocabulary list of useless nouns had expanded to include verbs and grammatical structure, coupled with some basic Salvadoran slang: "volado" instead of "cosa" for thing, "paja" instead of "mentira" for lie, "va pues" instead of "esta bien" for okay. I was feeling very good and very at home, but I still wanted to go and explore El Salvador. In order to do that, I'd have to get over my fear of walking the streets of San Salvador alone and further trust God for my safety. If I wanted to get out into the countryside, I would have to be brave and strong because I would have to ride the bus.

I think I must have prayed for an hour off and on while getting ready to ride my first bus. I was determined to go to the University of Central America (UCA) and see the rose garden I had read about. I knew I had to take the 21 into San Salvador and then switch to the 42 to make it to the university. I hadn't ever gone anywhere alone in this country, even though I had lived there four months by that time. I had always been flanked by other missionaries or my fellow teachers. I was never alone; it wasn't safe. After all, I don't know how many times I had heard that being a gringa, white girl, meant I was a target. But I hadn't come to El Salvador to hang out with other Americans; I had wanted to live in El Salvador with Salvadorans.

I walked out of my room and up the road. People did stop and look at me. I dropped my head and walked to the depot. So far so good. Someone cat-called me, and I lost my nerve, walked as nonchalantly as possible over to a shack, and asked the lady to sell me a Coke. I thought having something in my hand would give me something to focus on, make me look more like I belonged. Unfortunately, not having been out before, I had walked to the wrong shack. She didn't have any Coke, and I'd have to walk back to the store I'd passed a few minutes ago. I stood there for a while looking into the shack, smiling at the children who were playing on the dirt floor. I made a silly face at them, which made them laugh. The lady told me again she was sorry she had no Coke to sell me, but the store up the road did. I knew I had to continue my journey.

I remember self-consciously traveling the last couple of minutes to the bus stop, all of the rules I had heard rolling over in my mind: *You better look both ways before crossing the street, and if you see a car or bus in the distance,* stop *because they* will *speed up to run you over. Do* not *look a man in the eyes, or you will be inviting him into your bed. Do not let anyone see where your money is hidden, or you will be robbed and left on the streets alone.* And ironically, the final sage piece of advice: *Don't show fear, or you will be attacked.*

So I crossed the street to the bus depot, with my head down so as not to flirt, my head up, so I wouldn't look scared, unconsciously touching my pocket where my one hundred cólones were hiding, looking both ways before crossing the street, then quickly down again because a man happened to be on my left side as I watched for traffic, then up again to show I wasn't scared, and then, mercifully, I arrived, only to be surrounded by a group of bus drivers who had been watching the whole schizophrenic episode.

"Hey, hot mama, how are you today?"
"Pretty white girl, come over here."
"Curvy woman, I want you."
"You're looking good, baby."

All the while, they encircled me and looked me up and down, licking their lips, and acting the parts of the lustful hedonists I had been warned about so many times. I jumped into the first bus that opened its door, but as luck would have it, it wasn't due to depart for ten more minutes, since it was afternoon. I decided to look out the window and onto the street in the opposite direction of the bus drivers. Unfortunately, one of them approached me, pried open the window, and began talking to me, taunting me, telling me I was beautiful, just look at my eyes.

He prattled on that he'd never seen eyes like mine; how he wanted to kiss me and hold me and sleep with me. I decided to look down again and pray that the ten minutes would please hurry up and pass. Then a couple of my tormenters got on the bus and sat next to me, squeezed up against me, and continued the verbal assault. I couldn't move, and I didn't understand all they were saying, so I just sat and stared forward. They laughed at me for being a mute, for not looking at them. One said I was stuck up, and since I wasn't that pretty, I had no right to act like that.

I had never been as relieved as I was when the driver got in the bus and started the engine. The other bus drivers were forced to debark and leave me alone, but not before blowing kisses at me and laughing.

I should have recognized the start of my day as an

omen because I quickly got lost in Centro—downtown San Salvador. I had followed my directions and stepped out into traffic enough to flag down the right bus but not get run over. I had asked the cobrador if the bus went to the UCA by just repeating "UCA, UCA, UCA?" He had nodded and pulled me onto the bus because it had not fully stopped to pick me up, and I needed help with my footing. But he had either lied to me or hadn't heard me, I don't know which. All I know is, at the end of the ride when everyone debarked and he told me I had to get off, I burst into tears, and he asked me what was wrong. I just kept repeating, "UCA, UCA, UCA," and when he saw that I really was lost and scared, he took pity on me and took my hand and led me out of his bus and put me on the right one. I never did get to thank him for that, but he was my hero that day.

I eventually made it to the UCA and arrived home again through the generosity and kindness of people on the street who felt bad for the wandering, bewildered gringa who couldn't decide between looking up or looking down, touching the money she carried or ignoring it, deciding to cross the street or wait a little longer.

That was my first experience on the buses in El Salvador and with the cobradores from route 21, and I was not eager to repeat it. The next time I did, it wasn't much better. We got into a wreck in San Marcos when our bus driver pulled out into traffic, not having looked to see if that red car was too close or not. Everyone but me got off the bus quickly, which should have been my clue, but I didn't know where I was and only knew I was to stay on the 21 to reach downtown. The driver and cobrador looked back at me and cursed me for staying on the bus, which was unnerving, but since they didn't force me to go, I sat still.

What ensued next was a scene straight out of some crazy, spastic foreign film, where reality is suspended, and chaos rules the day. After the initial impact, everyone was yelling at each other. People on the street began to scatter; a lady selling French bread out of a big basket pulled her goods onto the sidewalk and crossed herself as Catholics do. We pulled out a second time and hit the car again, but this time on purpose. The driver of the car sped up and slammed into the bus. Back and forth we drove like unhinged bumper cars slamming into each other, regaining position, and then, *bam,* another hit. When the car broke off the mirror on the driver's side door of the bus, the cobrador had had enough. He pulled out a gun and flashed it at the driver. When the car driver saw the gun, he turned his steering wheel into the opposite direction and disappeared down a side street.

The cobrador and bus driver congratulated each other and laughed. "Did you see his face? Ha ha ha. He was scared! That son of a bitch didn't know anything. He acted just like a scared woman."

They had forgotten about me crouched down in my seat, holding onto the railing for dear life. But when they saw me, their expressions changed. "Hey, gringa, you didn't see anything, right?"

And me responding rather meekly in my bad Spanish, "Yo no veo nada, nada, nada." [29]

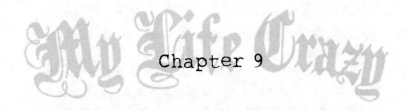

Chapter 9

I grew relatively accustomed to the bus drivers looking at me and making their comments. They had become bored with the total aggression package and settled for mere cat-calling without much else. I learned the bus routes and spent time in the streets of San Salvador practicing my Spanish, bargaining for vegetables in the market, and enjoying adventures into town.

Every day, my passion increased for the country. Life was so real and extreme there that I wanted to feel it with all five senses. I smelled the exhaust of the buses and the urine-stained walls, but also the ocean breeze with its scent of coconut and mango. I saw the broken people with devastated souls and bodies begging for money, but also the couples totally in love, kissing without any embarrassment, and the child with open, innocent eyes, envisioning himself as a king.

I heard the yells of the cobradores seeking passengers, the deafening sounds of salsa and rap pouring from monster-sized speakers, but also the placid suckling of a baby at her mother's young breast, and the sweet nothings being whispered into a lover's ear. I felt the assault of the sun on my face, burning me and making me tired, the hand of someone grabbing my arm in passing, but also the caress of the Pacific's tropical wind as it soothed my sunburn, and the patience of people trying with all their hearts to understand what I was desperate to communicate.

I tasted bitter oranges and soup cooked with chicken feet, but also the luscious delight of a mango that drenched my chin with its juice and the hot fried goodness of a pupusa stuffed with cabbage relish as it slipped down my throat, satiating my hunger. My life was happy, and my routine set, teaching classes and learning El Salvador, until God had something else to show me.

I was having my quiet time with God, praying and reading the Bible, when the number 21 came to my mind very strongly. I congratulated God on his good insight; those bus drivers needed a lot of prayer, and I would pray for them. I felt very pious praying for their salvation and repentance. They were awful people, and I was very saintly to pray for them. But soon, the prayers seemed insufficient, and I felt in my heart I was supposed to do more.

"God, I can't risk that. I mean, I am a missionary, and they are gross men. I'm not going to talk to them. I can't talk to them. I don't *want* to talk to them. My reputation will be ruined, and *you* wouldn't want that. My work wouldn't be accomplished here; I know you aren't serious. I can't take coffee to them. I won't take coffee to them! They will think I'm crazy or that I like them. I'm sure I'm confusing what I'm feeling you want. It is just some weird lack of sleep or tropical ailment... no! No! *No!*"

And without audible words, I knew in my heart, I had to go. The next day I made about three pots of coffee and poured them into a large pitcher. I had some sweet bread and sugar as well, placed them all into a bag, and made the walk up the road. My stomach was in knots, and I felt dreadful. I knew this was insanity; who took coffee to these guys? No one. They were horrible and undeserving, and of all the people in El Salvador, they were the only ones who scared me.

I got up to the bus depot, and the usual round of cat-calling began. Well, I would have none of it. I was not going to give these men coffee and bread for being so disrespectful. It went against everything I felt inside of me. So, I got on the bus, drove all the way into town, debarked, walked the couple of blocks to the next bus pick-up, and drove all the way home. It took over an hour, but it was worth it if I didn't have to share my coffee and bread. What was the saying, throwing your pearls before swine? When I got back to my room, I threw up from a combination of nerves and irritation.

I felt sick all day, and I couldn't shake the feeling that I *had* to deliver that coffee. I told God I would try again the next day. And I did, and I failed. I actually repeated the above scenario three times, and three times, I went home and threw up and was ill, before I actually had the nerve to ask the fatal question: "Do you want coffee?"

On that day, Abram, the dispatcher, limped into the depot and took his seat behind the three-legged table. He prepared the books for yet another day of microbuses, passengers, loud drivers, and crude, gangly cobradores. Abram often shook his head and commented on the young cobradores' attitudes and their lack of pride in being Indian.

He had lost part of his leg in the war when he had fought as a guerrilla for the people. He proudly wore red and felt happy seeing the FMLN posters covering his office—the whole depot. He religiously cleaned the urine stains off them and made sure they didn't get ripped by the hundreds of people who passed by every day. He wanted to believe the FMLN would fulfill their promises in the legislative assembly; he wanted to know he had not lost his leg in vain.

As Abram prepared for the day, a few buses pulled up to the bus stop. A driver relieved himself on the wall adjacent to the depot. His cobrador hawked up a lugey, and it landed a few feet from the driver. The shouts of "asshole" and "moron" had already begun. It was five in the morning. Abram yelled at them to shut up. He shook his head and finished penciling in the bus schedule.

At eight, when I walked to the bus depot, my stomach tightened again and my face flushed. Ten or so of the bus drivers began talking, and some even circled me like vultures eyeing roadkill. The bag I carried felt heavier than it was, and I contemplated turning back yet again.

Abram looked out from his building and told me the bus was about to leave, and I needed to get on it. I just shook my head, no. A driver explained to me that there was nothing to wait for, that the two buses were taking the only routes available, and I needed to board. Again I refused, and the sexual comments took a decided turn as the drivers started questioning my sanity.

I moved in closer to the depot and peered in, forcing myself to speak. I asked if they would like some coffee. Abram asked me when. I said now, that I had it in my bag. I pulled out the two-liter container and began pouring the coffee into the mugs I had packed. The silence that followed was overwhelming. We stood around staring at each other, not knowing what to say.

After they had finished, Abram asked how much he owed. I told him it was free, that it was a thank you for the work they did, and that Jesus loved them. The tension was broken by a few chuckles, and the questions began. Yes, I lived down the road. I was from the United States. I wanted them to know Jesus loved them. I was twenty-four. No, my Spanish wasn't that good.

When I packed up the dirty mugs and empty container, I said goodbye. I felt their stares on my back as I walked away. They called after me, "See you tomorrow," and I knew I had just become the new coffee service for the boys on route 21.

Chapter 10

"What's up with the white girl, man? It doesn't really make sense, does it?" Gusano took a drag of his cigarette and flicked the ashes to the ground. He looked at Panda for a response.

"She's pretty, man ... Maybe she's looking for a boyfriend. You know that white girls only come here looking for fun and action. Maybe she's one of those girls. That would be cool." They both laughed and walked over to the bus depot where I was and accepted the coffee I was pouring.

"Good morning. How are you?"

"I'm good, and you?"

"Good ... thanks for the coffee, all right?"

"You're welcome."

My Spanish wasn't much better than that at this point, so my conversations were short and to the point. I couldn't understand what they were saying about me when they peered into the depot where Abram shared his desk with me and my coffee mugs. I knew they were talking about me because they stared at me, made a comment to someone, and the two or three guys laughed or high-fived one another, and then they stared again.

Abram talked to me calmly and slowly every day for the hour it typically took to dispense the food and coffee. He asked me questions about myself, explained the political stories in the newspaper when I recognized someone's name from my studies or a political flag or symbol in the background of a photo, and he put the slang everyone spoke into the words I could look up in the dictionary.

He was very patient with me, leaning in to hear me stutter over my words, always trying to fill in the blanks for me when I paused too long, unable to capture the phrase in Spanish that floated around my brain in English. He could have been a teacher with his ability to lead me through a conversation, prompting me with questions or comments, applauding me when I voiced an entire thought correctly.

He told me to ignore the lewd comments from the bus drivers. When I told him I didn't understand, he told me that was a good thing. He hit the iron bars that protected the windows of the depot with his rolled-up newspaper when the comments got too bad. He looked at me, rolled his eyes, and said the one word he knew in English: "crazy."

It was during that first week of taking coffee to them that I met the cockiest, most arrogant cobrador ever. He looked different from the rest of them with his Nike baseball cap pulled low over his eyes. His baggy khakis and oversized football jersey, coupled with his white tennis shoes, made him look bigger than he actually was. His fingers never seemed to stop moving; they were going through some sort of pattern over and over as he leapt off his bus and swaggered over to the depot where I was. He handed his notepad filled with the bus schedule to Abram. He ignored me for a moment, then turned his head to the side, tilted his chin toward me, looked at me from under the brim of his hat with one eyebrow raised over his light brownish-yellow eyes, and then laughed a little mockingly.

"Whatever," was all he said before he walked away without another look at me.

"Who's that?" I asked Abram.

"That crazy guy is Gato. He's in the gang and is very bad."

I was a little scared to find out he was a gang member, since the first and only other time I had encountered a gang member, he had threatened me. I remember I had walked up to buy pupusas at one of the little shacks. It had been around six thirty in the evening and getting dark. I placed my order and sat down to wait across from a young man. He looked a little sinister as he kept his head low, looking back and forth at all the people passing by, glaring at them. He flashed some sign, which prompted a little boy next to me to ask him if he was a gang member.

"Yeah ... from the Mara Salvatrucha, man."

The boy was impressed and started asking questions. What was it like to be in the gang? Was it fun? What did they do? Had he killed anyone? Did you get a lot of girlfriends in the gang? Trompeta, the gang member, had been flattered by all the attention the boy was giving him. He had answered most of the questions in a serious tone and then mentioned that sometimes the girlfriend issue got complicated if a gangster was dating another gangster. The boy's mouth fell open.

"There are girls in the gang? What do they do?"

Trompeta laughed and looked around, allowing his angry eyes to settle on mine. "Yeah, there are girls in the gang, and they—" he paused for dramatic effect "—kill white girls."

It got pretty quiet as soon as he said that, and the little boy told me I should go, and that he would bring me my pupusas when they were done. He was worried for me. I was taken aback by what Trompeta had said and his firm and penetrating gaze. My mind raced with possibilities: should I run away, should I ask him why he would say such a thing, should I laugh, or should I act like I hadn't heard? Without really giving myself a chance to process all my options, I shoved out my hand and stuck it in his face.

"Wow, look, I'm shaking. I'm very scared of you. Are you happy now?"

We sat staring each other down for a couple of minutes, my heart beating entirely too fast, and then he burst out laughing.

"You're crazy … but cool. You're all right," he said as he shook my hand and assured me no one would kill me, at least not from *his* clique.

So while Gato's gang status did scare me a little, I was intrigued by him and his obvious show of disdain for me. He was trying too hard not to like me before he had even talked to me, and I loved a challenging kid. I liked that he was the only one of them who had not flirted with me, cat-called me, or tried to get close to me. In fact, he was the only one who had been rude to me up to that point, and he reminded me of some of my students back in the States ... the ones with foul attitudes who felt that anyone older was a threat and someone to be distrusted. I liked him instantly.

The next time I saw him, I was determined to make him talk to me. When he got off his bus, the rap music blaring, he looked both ways across the street and spit on the ground after clearing his throat. I smiled as he approached, and he just scrunched his brow in irritation at my audacity to look at him directly.

"Hi, Gato. How are you?"

"Fine," he responded without looking at me.

"Would you like some coffee or sweetbread?"

He looked at me for a couple of minutes, annoyed by the intrusion I was making into his morning routine, before answering, "No, no thanks."

He then walked over to Comedor Tita, bought a cup of coffee, and walked back in front of me and drank it. He looked directly at me as he finished his last sip and smiled. I laughed to myself. I loved this kid. He was challenging me, and I gladly accepted.

I simply responded to him as he had responded to me the first time I had met him: "Whatever." And this time he laughed.

I asked God, in my quiet times, to help me understand this Gato. He was interesting and different, but I felt something in my heart for him that I had never felt before. I felt a protective love, a completely pure sense of responsibility for him, and a claim on my heart for time, attention, and loyalty. I felt it almost immediately after meeting him. In the quiet times, I felt God confirming the love I had for him. I needed to get to know him if it was the only thing I did during my time in El Salvador. I couldn't really explain why Gato stood out to me from everyone else I met, but he did. I felt a burden for him, a need to pray for him, to get to know him, and to love him. So I sought him out, making small talk, attempting to understand him. And in the beginning, our conversations went a little like this:

"You're crazy, right? Why do you bring us coffee? I think you are either crazy … or … well, I won't even say it."

"It's just that I want to show you God's love in this simple way … and I want to be a friend."

"So you are crazy," he laughed and then told me he had to go and he'd drink my coffee tomorrow. I waved goodbye to him as he got on his bus and took off down the road. He smiled a little as he passed me by, a little embarrassed that he had talked to me and let down his guard. We began talking for longer periods of time, although I had a hard time understanding his Spanish, and he wasn't very sympathetic about it. I could tell he was warming up to me. He thought I was odd, but funny. He also liked the fact that a lot of the other bus drivers wanted to have me spend time with them, and I was choosing to spend as much time as I could with him. Gato would tease them.

"I'm so handsome; you all wish you could be half as good-looking as me. It's cool that the gringa is always looking for me. You know it's because I am just so irresistible. What can I say?"

I continued to love him and feel the need to protect him, even though I still knew very little about him.

One day when he arrived at the depot, he placed his hand on the bars while waiting for Abram to fill out his bus schedule. He said hi to me, and I offered him coffee. He declined, telling me his stomach hurt and that coffee would make him sicker. He continued to hold onto the window bars, laughing with the other bus drivers who were hanging around drinking coffee, when I lost another battle with God. I felt compelled to grab his hand and hold it there, while I said a silent prayer for his safety. I really would have preferred to pray elsewhere and not grab onto his hand, but I also remembered being sick for three days when I had disobeyed another one of God's urgings. So I begrudgingly wrapped my hand around his and started to pray silently. And because the bus drivers still did not know me well, this hand grabbing only fueled the speculation about my sanity.

"Ahhh yes, you were right. She isn't all there..."

"What is wrong with this girl? Do you think she's in love with Gato?"

"That stupid son of a bitch... how did he get her?"

"Maybe she really is crazy; what do you think?"

Gato tried to pull his hand away for a second, but when I wouldn't let him go, he relaxed and let me finish what he could not hear and did not understand, but was trying to. I finished the prayer, continued holding his hand, and announced, "I love you, Gato."

Gato just chuckled and said, "Yep." A loud shout of surprise and laughter escaped the men hanging around, and some rushed to correct my obvious mistake. Love is a precious thing … something not just thrown around to whomever. I just smiled, my attention focused on Gato, whose hand I still held firmly against the bars of the depot. "No, Gato, I love you." And everyone shook their heads and agreed that something was wrong with me. My coffee was good and all, but what was I thinking with this new revelation?

"She's in love with Gato … this just doesn't make sense."

But when Gato had his hand free and boarded his bus to leave for Centro, calling out for passengers and collecting bus fare, he knew that something was different with this gringa. She wasn't his girlfriend. She wasn't his type, and he wasn't hers, yet something was going on, and he wanted to know what it was. He was intrigued.

Chapter 11

I had been taking coffee to the bus drivers for several months by now, and my love for Gato and the burden to help him and serve him in some capacity was overwhelming. Unfortunately, I still couldn't understand a word of the slang Gato said to me. When he began to speak to me beyond the polite necessities and basic words I knew, I was lost. His use of símon, chále, neta,[30] and all the rest of it completely blew my mind. Even though I wrote down the words to look up, I couldn't find them in the dictionary. I told him that he would need to explain what he was saying in other words, and he laughed and said he didn't know any other way to talk. So he and I were at a linguistic impasse, and I needed some help.

I heard about a church that had a gang ministry, and they were always looking for entry into different cliques to spread the message of salvation. I contacted them and told them I took coffee to bus drivers, that seven of the cobradores were gang members, and that I needed help. They gladly accepted, so now I had partners.

I stood at the desvio[31] feeling quite small and a little stupid because my new ministry partners, Soledad and Samuel, had asked me to take them down to the bus depot to meet these gang members I knew. They said they would help me lug the coffee and sweet bread there in order to meet Gato and ask permission to meet with his homeboys.

My friends were growing impatient as I made small talk with the bus drivers and poured them coffee. We were enjoying our usual ritual and thought nothing of it. I suppose for someone new to the scene, it would seem annoyingly long. My guests asked me several times when Gato was due to arrive. Abram said Gato would be there any minute. He had said the same thing for the last half an hour. I just smiled and poured the next cup of coffee. When the bus pulled up, Gato got off and walked over to the depot to find out the bus schedule for his driver. He saw me and smiled. I smiled back and asked him if he wanted some coffee. He politely took the coffee and then noticed the tattoo behind Samuel's ear: 213. It was for the Los Angeles area code, but Gato thought the 13 in it was associated with la Mara Salvatrucha.

"Cool," he smiled and winked at me, showing his approval.

Samuel started up an easy conversation with Gato, having shared a similar experience. Besides being Salvadoran and poor, they were both gang members. Gato asked about the 213 tattoo and then grew angry.

Samuel had been in 18th Street, the MS rival. Gato poured the coffee he had been drinking onto the ground and handed the mug back to me. "This penocho[32] is going to come here to talk to me? You are out of your mind!" He started to walk away but looked back and saw my pathetic expression—a mixture of embarrassment and apology. He looked at me, pensively, for a long time, and then reluctantly turned around to finish the conversation.

I remember his look. He didn't understand how I could insult him in this way, but there was this sense of compassion and loyalty to me that compelled him to stay there and hear my friend out. He'd later tell me it had been a hard decision for him, but that ultimately, he hadn't wanted to embarrass me by leaving.

They sold Jesus pretty hard to him for fifteen minutes, telling Gato he had to accept today, right now, without hesitation, because no one ever knows when they will die. I felt uncomfortable because I didn't think Jesus *had* to be sold. Wouldn't one just want to know him if one had seen his love in action? But they were Salvadoran and knew the culture far better than I ever would, so I just hung back and watched the sales pitch.

I was acutely aware of the time. Gato only had forty-five minutes to eat breakfast until he had to work again. He wouldn't know when his next break would be until later. He was down to thirty minutes. I heard them ask him if he wanted to accept Christ as his savior. He actually asked them what the time was first. They told him, and he said he would be glad to ask Christ into his heart. I started to laugh, but was instantly hushed by the serious and fervently dedicated looks of my friends. Gato looked at me with an amused expression on his face. My friends thought their oratory had worked, and that the Holy Spirit had moved within Gato. I knew he was just hungry and wanted to get away from them. But I shut my mouth and watched as they began to pray with him.

Gato repeated the prayer as he leaned up against the depot wall. I just stood watching him from about three yards off. The prayer was long and zealously prayed. I felt great compassion for my partners in ministry at that moment because they really believed Gato had made a solemn decision. Midway through the prayer, Gato looked over at me, smiled, and winked. I started to laugh, and he had to fight back his laughter in order to get through the prayer. He actually caught his chuckle in his throat and coughed. They prayed that God would heal his sore throat.

When they were finished and the final amen said, they both hugged him and welcomed him into the family of God. He shook their hands and went into the little diner to eat. I followed him with my eyes. He looked out at me through the wire enclosure and smiled while shaking his head. I blew him a kiss.

As we walked back to my house, I told my companions that Gato had been faking everything.

"I don't think Gato meant what he prayed. It didn't seem real."

"How are you going to believe that, Kylla? Perhaps you have little faith."

"But he was looking at me during the prayer and laughing."

"Well, nobody can say those words and not be saved. So your friend is now your brother ... you just have to have faith."

I admired their ability to convince themselves

that Gato was saved from anything. Despite the language barrier, I knew him well enough to know that what had just transpired had been a joke. Gato was no different than he had been before he repeated their prayer. But even though the message of salvation fell on deaf ears, they had been able to get one thing from Gato—an invitation to meet the other boys from his clique. We would be going next week.

Chapter 12

I was so excited to meet the other gang members. I woke up early that morning and made the coffee and drank almost a whole pot myself. I wanted to see where this meeting would take the ministry, but I was also desperate to understand Gato. He was so attached to his gang and was willing to die for them. I needed to see where his heart was.

Gato met us at the depot, and we boarded the bus together. When we got to the Ceiba, it looked fairly deserted. I saw a woman selling hot dogs from a little cart she owned. I also saw some church-goers, but I didn't see anyone who looked like Gato, bagged out and flashing signs. I looked at Gato with suspicion. He rolled his eyes at me, and we got off the bus. Gato was acting very formally with Samuel, Soledad, and me. He kept making sure we were okay, acting as a tour guide, explaining all the different places and people. We tagged along behind him on this museum tour. He led us around the backside of the Ceiba to an alleyway. A couple of gang members walked up, shook hands with Gato, and flashed their signs. Gato introduced them to each one of us and said we had something to say to them. The boys sat down on the pavement, and Samuel began to preach to them by giving them his testimony. Gato walked over and stood by me.

He whispered in my ear jokingly, "Isn't it true I

no longer have to listen to the message? I'm already a convert. I'm a brother in the faith."

"Gatito, you must think I'm stupid." I laughed. "Yeah, you need to listen to the message, but I know you aren't ready to accept it, or am I wrong?

"You're smart, I'll give you that. I will die a gang member, and if God really loved me, he wouldn't have given me the life I have had."

"How so?"

"Nah, I'm not going to tell you anything right now. Talk to these guys. I'm out of here."

And he left. I focused on Samuel's testimony and on one of the boys who was sitting and listening with rapt attention. He sat frozen during that first meeting. I didn't know who he was. He didn't look like a gang member. He seemed sad. His eyes were huge and dog-like. He ignored the distractions of people walking up and down the street, of his homies[33] making jokes and cat-calling women as they passed by. He just sat there, not speaking.

I asked him what his name was. He told me it was Jaime, but his tag was Killer. He smiled at me, but his eyes were devastatingly sad. He told me his mom and sisters were Christians. He said he'd heard all of this before. I asked why he was listening. He told me it was like God was talking to him, and he had to listen.

He asked if we would come to his house and talk to his family because he wanted to go to the rehabilitation home for gang members that Samuel had mentioned. He was only seventeen, so he needed to let his family know where he was going.

He led us to his home. We wound around dirt paths. They were barely large enough for a car to pass on; some of them *weren't* big enough, and we had to get out of Soledad's car and walk. The cliff that overlooked his house was also the path that led to it. We half-climbed, half-slid, down the hillside. There was nothing to grip. Jaime laughed at the sight of me trying to make it down without slipping. I was unsuccessful. I laughed too.

We made it to the house, a two-room building with dirt floors in 18ᵗʰ Street territory. I found that odd, since Jaime was a member of the MS. His mom came out to greet us. She offered us a drink of freshly-squeezed lemonade, which tasted great after the climbing fiasco. Jaime explained who we were and asked if he could go and live in the rehab home.

His mother was nervous and began asking questions about the house and the church that supported it. When she was satisfied with the answers, she gave her blessing. Jaime packed up a couple of outfits and left to begin a new life away from the gang.

The home was located in Mejicanos, a sector not known for its gentleness or wealth. The state penitentiary was located there as well, and the area's tough reputation preceded it.

The home itself was a small, three-room structure. One room served as both kitchen and bathroom. The bathroom was separated from the kitchen by only a half wall. The other two rooms served both as bedrooms and living room. During the day, the boys propped the mattresses up against the wall so they could watch television. There were twelve boys living there when Jaime arrived.

The boys came from all four gangs in El Salvador: the Mao Mao, La Maquina, and of course, the two largest, 18th Street and Mara Salvatrucha. Each young man had made a choice to walk away from his clique to become a Christian. They lived in the rehab house in an effort to get off drugs and learn to take care of themselves.

The leaders of the home were themselves ex-gang members. They had been out of the gangs for several years and were studying in a seminary. It was part of their curriculum, a ministry on the streets. The leaders took their jobs seriously, assigning the new recruits chores and overseeing the general activity of the home. They led Bible studies and prayed with each one of the boys.

When Jaime arrived, he was immediately welcomed into the home. He was given a sleeping assignment, instructed on the rules of the home, and introduced to the other residents. While it was a bit unnerving for him when he saw how many 18th Street members were there, he calmed down when they warmly welcomed him as a brother.

I went to visit Jaime the following week. He was doing well and enjoying the studies they were doing. He was getting a little fatter, since he liked the food and was thrilled he could have as much as he wanted. Jaime wanted to visit the guys in his clique to tell them about this place and God. The leaders were against it because he had only arrived a week earlier. They didn't think he was ready to face the temptations of gang life and be able to resist them. I agreed.

When Jaime did get permission to leave the home, he went back to Santo Tomas to see his homies. When they noticed how good he looked and how happy he seemed, several of them wanted to go to the home with Jaime when he returned. I became a little nervous when I heard them talking, since the risk of failure was great for an entire group of friends attempting to change together. There was a major potential for an all-or-nothing result. If they all liked it and did well, they would all stay; but likewise, if one got angry or offended, there was a threat of all of them quitting together out of loyalty to the one. Samuel disagreed, believing the boys were sincere. Since he was Salvadoran himself, I acquiesced, and seven members of the MS clique loaded up their belongings and went to the home. Gato was not one of them.

Within a week, the grumbling began. The group of boys from Santo Tomas was separating itself from everyone else. They were picking on some of the members of 18th Street who were there, taking their food, hiding their things, bullying them. The boys were getting bored and defying the rules. By the end of the second week, they all left the home, and Jaime went with them.

Throughout the two years I was in Santo Tomas, Jaime would appear at my door. He would talk to me, cry, go to church for a month at a time, talk about making a real change in his life, and tell me how much he wanted God. These times with Jaime seemed sincere. However, jail time, fights with 18th Street, or rejection of God and re-embracing of his MS homeboys always followed.

Jaime was a constant struggle for me. I loved him and wanted to believe him. I wanted the best for him. Every time he'd come and tell me he wanted to change, I tried to help. Every time he'd return to the streets, I was crushed. He seemed so defeated, and his eyes remained sad. His heart was much the same, and I never could get through to him. I failed.

When I left El Salvador, I saw Jaime, bandana on his head, pacing back and forth in the Ceiba. He was flashing gang signs and laughing with his homies. He happened to look up to see me pass by. I waved resignedly; he sat down and put his head in his hands. Without a word being spoken, our entire relationship had been summed up in that final moment.

Chapter 13

I was in the Ceiba talking with Salvatrucha members when Gato came up and sat next to me. I asked him how he was, and he said he was good.

"I've got to talk to you," he whispered.

I told him we could talk now. He just shook his head no and continued to make small talk with me. The other gang members wandered around flashing signs and joking with each other. A group of guys sat back in their baggy clothes with their baseball caps pulled down low to cover their eyes and watched the girls who walked by. You could hear the "mamacitas lindas" and "preciosas"[34] being whispered seductively to the girls they saw. The girls smiled but ducked their heads and walked faster.

Gato and I watched the scene for a time, the guys so cool and confident and the girls shy yet flattered. Gato even threw in a couple of cat-calls for good measure. I always teased him about the amount and intensity of cat-calls the Salvadoran men could produce. He thought it was funny that I analyzed it.

"That's how it is here, Kylla. The girls are hot and we're men, so what do you expect?"

"I'm just saying it's different in my country. When I wander around in the States, nobody's cat-calling, 'Mamacita linda, chelita mia, ven aca.'"[35]

"You're crazy, Kylla." He laughed heartily at the

imitation I gave. "I'm not going to say anything to you, okay? You don't have to feel uncomfortable with me."

"Well, awesome, do I have your word?"

"Of course."

"Cool." I smiled, and Gato smiled back. Our deal had been made, and I knew he would stick to it.

"Hey, I still need to talk to you."

"Okay, talk."

"Not here, wait a minute."

I didn't understand why he wouldn't just talk to me in front of everyone. So I asked him what the big mystery was. He grabbed my hand and walked me over to the other side of the plaza where the Antel phone company was located. I leaned against the wall, and Gato started to whisper.

"Look, Oso is sick. He needs help, and I was thinking you could help, but only if you want to." I asked what the symptoms were, and he told me that Oso had major stomach cramps so severe he couldn't even get out of bed. He was in pain, and no one had money to do anything about it.

I told Gato to take me to Oso immediately. We got on a bus and headed out to Santiago Texacu-ango where the destroyer was located. On the way, I got off at my house, changed clothes, and grabbed some money. I had been wearing shorts, and I knew it wouldn't help my credibility with the doctors if I didn't change into a dress. Hanging out with gang members and *looking* juvenile would have stopped us from getting into the hospital.

It was sunset as we made our way up the hill and around the bend. We walked for a long time, and after so many twists and turns, I had no idea how to get back onto the main road. This scared me a little because I had only known Oso and Gato for a short time. It was intimidating to be walking into a situation where I would have no help if something were to go wrong.

I smelled the smoke and urine from several yards away. Someone had been smoking marijuana and cigarettes. I knew we must be near the house where they lived. By this time, I couldn't see anything. The sun was gone and the path before me was black. I tripped over some thorny branches and cut myself on my knee. I lifted my dress and strained my eyes to see anything at all.

As we closed the distance to the house, I heard the heavy metal music in the background and smelled the smoke more acutely. As I tripped over several empty bottles of liquor and beer, my stomach twisted into knots. I must admit, I wondered if Gato had been told to bring me to the shack as a sacrifice of some sort. I was growing more frightened. I hesitated outside the shack, but Gato told me to come inside.

I entered a small room. Two beds covered the entire floor. One bed had several gang members, stoned and bemused, sitting on its corners. Oso lay on the other bed, pale and still. A girl was in the bed with him. She was on top of him, kissing him, her bra discarded on the floor.

She turned her head toward me and laughed. "So

this is the white girl that hangs out in the Ceiba?"
Casting a disapproving glance over my body, she bent
down and whispered something in Oso's ear. Then,
laughing, she started kissing him again. Gato looked
at me, checking my face for any offense. I just felt stupid standing there, not knowing what to do.

Oso finally spoke and greeted me after about five
minutes of silence that seemed like an eternity. I told
him I was here to take him to the doctor. He told me
he didn't need to go. His girlfriend laughed at me for
having shown up for nothing and told me to leave.
Gato got mad when she spoke to me again. He yelled
at her, "Shut up, bitch!" and she slunk back. No one
defended her, not even Oso. I wondered how she must
have felt at that moment.

Gato turned his attention to Oso, urging him, telling him he needed to get some medicine so he could
be back in fighting shape. Oso agreed. The drunk and
stoned gang members nodded their approval as well.
Oso's girlfriend covered herself with a blanket and
told Oso to go with me.

I looked at her and thanked her. I was embarrassed
for her as she sat half-naked in front of all those guys
who talked to her however they wanted. She dropped
her head and stared at the floor. Gato helped pull Oso
out of bed. The other gang members handed Oso his
shoes after his girlfriend put a shirt on him. Then
Gato and I flanked Oso and were off into the night.

When we arrived at the hospital, which was in
18th Street territory and not the safest place to be with
two MS gang members, the guard only allowed Oso

and me to enter. Gato had to wait outside by himself. We sat in the waiting room and talked about different things. He smiled at me and thanked me for helping him. He apologized for his girlfriend, but I shrugged and told him it was no big deal. The only other patients in the hospital were pregnant women. I teased Oso that perhaps he was in labor himself and that was the reason for his pains. He laughed and shook his head violently, "No way, woman … not me!"

The doctor called my name, and Oso and I went to the examining room where he was given a full exam. He had food poisoning. The doctor prescribed some medicine for him that started to help immediately. I paid, and we left. Before we made it to the gate where Gato was waiting, Oso stopped me and gave me an awkward hug. "Hey, thanks for helping me. When you need something, all you have to do is ask, okay?"

We walked to our respective homes. The earlier apprehension of possibly being attacked and killed had disappeared. When left alone with my thoughts, I realized how elated I felt that Gato had come to me with his concerns, even if he had been embarrassed to ask for help. He had never done that before, always being so careful about showing me any form of need or weakness. I was proud to see him overcome his pride to help a friend. I was being allowed a small glimpse into him, and I was truly contented. Although that night was never mentioned again, a trust had begun on both sides. Gato began to trust me more, and I him. We were never nervous or scared around each other again.

Chapter 14

I'd gone down to the Ceiba again to hang out with the gang members. After the night at the hospital something had shifted in the relationship between Gato and me. He felt very protective of me and made sure I was taken care of whenever I was in gang territory. Today, we were supposed to play basketball or something like that. I got there and sat alone, waiting. I hadn't quite mastered the "Latin time" concept. I kept showing up at the exact moment I was told to arrive. I always sat alone.

About twenty minutes into my wait, Oso, Loco, Gato, and several others arrived. They greeted each other and me. We covered the basic conversational questions and sat around talking. An old man selling ice cream hobbled by, ringing his bell. Gato, always the gentleman with me, asked if I would like one and handed me an ice cream cone before I could answer.

It was a quiet day in the Ceiba. A couple gang members I didn't know crossed the street and started talking to some kid who was waiting for the bus. I chatted with Gato, who was sitting next to me, and happily ate my ice cream. I soon noticed that all the guys around me had become deathly silent. I looked toward them; their attention was riveted across the street.

I watched the scene play out in slow motion

before my eyes. The gang members' voices started to get loud and angry. One of them reached down and brutally slapped the boy's head. I could hear him protesting, saying he was waiting for the bus, nothing more. The gang members began to kick and punch him. The kid tried to get to his feet, but they didn't let up. He scrambled away under the heavy hits he was taking. Blood splattered everywhere. One of the gang members pulled a knife from his pocket. His friend grabbed him by the shirt and told him no, that there were too many witnesses.

My ice cream had melted all over my hand and lap. I was stunned by what I was seeing. Instinctively, I started yelling at Gato to make the guys stop. He explained patiently, as if to a child, that there was nothing he could do. He grabbed some napkins and sopped up the ice cream that was all over me. "Kylla, you're dirty. Let me help you."

I wasn't even paying attention to him. I was in shock. After the beating ended, the gang members crossed back over to our side of the street. I demanded that they put the knife away. I was furious, as much with myself for having done nothing, as with them. I was yelling irately. The gang member with the knife pressed his face up to mine menacingly and told me to keep my mouth shut. Gato jumped up and got between us protectively. The tension escalated. I wasn't even thinking about the knife; I was furious. Oso rushed over, grabbed the knife-wielding gangster's shoulder and assured him I was cool and wouldn't say anything. Oso persuaded him to put the knife away. They took off together, while Gato stayed and, concerned, asked if I was okay.

The rest of the gang members fanned out and disappeared, and the bloodied boy hobbled to a bus and safety. I was left alone with Gato in the Ceiba, in a pool of ice cream and with a sickening feeling in my stomach. Gato, trying to make me feel better, told me not to worry, that everyone was alive and well. I was mad at him for his lack of power or control; I didn't know what to think.

He said he had to go in case the police showed up. Handing me the napkins and smiling at me, he said, "I'll talk to you in a little while, okay?" I nodded numbly and finished cleaning myself up. I just wished that what I had seen could be washed away as easily.

Chapter 15

"Does it bother you that we're here to help gang members leave your gang?" I sat next to Gato and looked at him questioningly, waiting for a response. He looked at me for a moment and then glanced at the ground before answering; when he did, he spoke in a whisper.

"Look, Kylla, if they want to leave this type of life behind and have a normal, peaceful life without problems and violence, it would be better for them. In the end, they are my family, not just my homeboys. I'm not going to stop them. So, no, it doesn't bother me; I support them."

"And why don't you want to change your life? You know we are prepared to do whatever you need to help you."

"I know ... but no ... there's no other life out there for me."

"I don't believe that."

"You don't have to believe it, but that's the way it is."

He looked at me for a second, and I dropped my gaze. I had talked to him about getting out of the gang so many times. And I knew there were things he wouldn't tell me about himself. I was frustrated because over time, the love I felt for him had only grown stronger. I wanted him to be happy, safe, and really okay, but sadly, nothing I did was making a difference.

"Look, here comes your pastor. I'm out."

Meanwhile my ministry partner, Samuel, had gotten off the bus at the Ceiba and was crossing the street to join me. We sat down on the bench and waited for some gang members to come by when Miguel Luis showed up. He was a handsome young man, tall and thin. He was MS, although I don't remember his tag because I never called him by it. He had introduced himself to us with his real name.

He listened to the short message given by Samuel and decided he wanted to know more about the Bible. He said he wanted to go live in the safehouse. He wanted to leave the gang and begin anew. He talked to me and asked if I lived in the rehab house as well. I told him I didn't, but that I visited twice a week. He seemed irritated by that, which I didn't understand, but continued talking to me anyway.

Two days later, Miguel Luis packed up his meager belongings and traveled to the rehab house. He asked me to come and see him soon. I assured him I would. I waved goodbye as the bus drove away.

Later that week I visited the home. Miguel seemed to be adjusting well. The home leader said Miguel was diligent with reading the Bible and participating in activities with the other young men. When he saw me, he smiled warmly, came over, and gave me a hug.

He told me he was having a hard time understanding the Bible. He wanted to figure it out and be able to answer everyone's questions, including his own. I told him to slow down and just spend time with God. He became agitated and would speak louder, shake his head, or drop it into his hands when I wouldn't answer his questions to his satisfaction. He told me he needed to know the answers now.

When it came time for me to leave, Miguel escorted me to the bus. He told me to come back soon and see him. I did, partly because I felt it was my responsibility, but also because I genuinely liked Miguel and the other boys in the home. Unfortunately, every visit, our conversations were typically the same. He still wanted me to give him immediate, concrete answers, and I couldn't.

I received an excited phone call from Miguel several weeks later. He had earned temporary leave privileges from the rehab home and was going home for the weekend to visit his family and friends and wanted me to come to his house with him. I accepted the heartfelt invitation to lunch. I was thrilled to know someone who was so excited about God after having left the gang. I was anxious to meet his family and spend time with Miguel outside the home. He told me he would pick me up at the bus stop to escort me to his house.

When I arrived at the depot, I noticed that Miguel was dressed in a white button-down shirt and striped tie. His hair was slicked back, and he had drenched himself in cologne. It surprised me he had taken such pains to look nice. I wasn't used to seeing him all dressed up. I complimented him on his appearance, and he blushed. We boarded the bus together and had a nice conversation about God. He motioned to me as we approached the stop we needed. The cobrador helped me off the bus, snickering because he knew what I was about to encounter even though I did not.

Climbing to the top of the hill, Miguel and I had to grab onto twigs and weeds, anything anchored to the ground, to steady ourselves on the steep ascent. I really regretted wearing my heels and a skirt and was silently chastising myself for my wardrobe choice. After five minutes of excruciating effort, I asked Miguel where he lived. He told me we were almost there.

Eventually we arrived at a mud shack. Bent and corroded pieces of metal made up the windows in the home. It had a dirt floor, a makeshift table, and an outside kitchen and bathroom; it was typical of many of the houses I'd seen in San Salvador. Miguel seemed immediately embarrassed when a chicken pecked at my feet, and I had to step over the half-starved dog that blocked the entrance to the kitchen. Because of malnutrition, it lacked the energy to move. I saw that Miguel was ashamed of his home, which made me feel bad. I grabbed his arm and told him I was excited to meet his family.

His father greeted me indifferently and left. Miguel's siblings ran about, chasing the chickens and playing tag. His mother embraced me wearily and welcomed me to her home. She apologized because she knew I was accustomed to more amenities. I assured her that her home was lovely and that family made a home, not things. She motioned to a chair at the table, and I sat down.

Miguel sat in the chair next to me, and the feast began. His mother and teenaged sister served steaming hot bean soup with cheese and warm tortillas. I was thankful for the delicious lunch, and it happened to be my absolute favorite meal in El Salvador. I was telling her so, when Miguel quieted me. His sister then brought us half a chicken each, along with a salad, more cheese, and rice.

Even though I was overly full, the food kept coming. Miguel's mom brought us a thick corn-meal drink, Atol, as the third course. I felt like I was going to throw up. Miguel was visibly shaken by my lack of interest in the drink, so I smiled and tried to drink more. His mother then served coffee and sweet bread. My stomach was taut and aching from the amount of food and drink I was pouring into it. Trying to hide my nausea, I thanked his mom for the wonderful meal and leaned back in my chair.

All through the meal my legs had been itching. When I looked down, I realized they were covered with bites and little black bugs. I tried maneuvering myself away from the table and the fleas that had taken up residence there. Miguel looked at me squirming and noticed my legs. He politely suggested we walk around. I could barely move with so much food residing in my belly, but decided it might save my legs, so I forced myself up from the chair.

We took a tour of his small shack. There was one mattress where, I assume, his parents slept. The floor was reserved for the children. There were no other furnishings besides the table and two chairs. His mom sat in the room on the other side of the kitchen. She pulled the other chair out for me, and I sat.

As she spoke, her conversation went into an interviewing mode. She wanted to know my background, my religious affiliations, and my age. She then began to tell me about how Miguel Luis was a serious boy, not given to many romances, and she wanted to make sure I was right for him. I sat in stunned silence. I had been unaware that this lunch had been an approval session for his parents. To my knowledge, I wasn't dating Miguel, nor did I have any interest in him that way.

Miguel stood over in the corner, dodging my questioning looks. He seemed a little embarrassed and a little guilty. He knew I had been ill-prepared for this interview. Feeling tremendously uncomfortable, I avoided his mother's more pointed questions and spoke in general terms of how Miguel would make a good husband for some girl someday. After a while, his mother realized my uneasiness. With a perplexed face, she looked at Miguel. He responded by rushing me out of his home and onto the bus.

We sat in silence on the trip home. I didn't know what to say. Part of me wanted to ask him what he had been thinking while the other half didn't want to touch the subject. I suppose he felt the same way as neither one of us spoke. We got to my home and said our goodbyes when Miguel handed me a slip of paper and gave me a hug. He loosened his tie, unbuttoned his shirt collar, and walked away, shaking his head dejectedly. I opened the paper and read the romantic poem with its border of hearts and flowers. At the bottom of the page, written in English, were the words "I love you."

Chapter 16

"It's uncool being out here with you." In the darkness and stillness of night, another missionary and I sat across from Antonio. The sixteen-year-old sat hunched over with a black baseball cap pulled down tightly over his forehead. I didn't know him. His mother, a lady who sold bread in my town, had set up the meeting. She had mentioned to me that her son was a member of the MS and said he wanted to hear about the rehabilitation house.

Antonio came from a Christian family. His younger brothers and sister were in the English classes I taught at school. They loved and supported Antonio. However, despite his good family life, Antonio had joined the gang because of his size and foul temper. He was big and muscular, and the gang—Gato in particular—had courted him.

As my friend and I sat across from him, we felt a little strange. It was late at night, and no one knew where we were. When Antonio had refused to meet us anywhere public, we had agreed to meet in a dark corner on a side street, so we were a little scared. I tried to shake it off and asked Antonio what his tag was. He told me it was Danger from Santomas. When I questioned why he should be called Danger, he smiled and said he liked to hit people. He was good at fighting, so the name fit. My friend and I laughed nervously, and I asked what he wanted from this meeting.

His story was atypical because he'd stayed in school, unlike most gang members, and wanted to finish his high school degree. He had joined the gang for "el vacil"[36] and enjoyed the pleasures the gang offered in the way of drugs, girls, and power. He had no intentions of being a gang member for the rest of his life. He wanted a calm life and a family. He had future plans. He said he was in a position where he was going to have to prove his loyalty to the gang again by committing a crime. He didn't want to do it. He wanted out but was not willing to suspend his schooling by going to a rehab house if he couldn't leave for school every day.

I told him about the rehab house, and when I mentioned he would have to postpone his studies for a short time, he stood up and thanked me for meeting with him. He couldn't commit to the rehab house without the promise of school. I told him I understood but to let me know if he changed his mind. He asked us to pray for him and not tell anyone about our meeting. We agreed to keep it to ourselves, and Danger disappeared into the night.

Danger was a big hitter in the Santo Tomas clique. He had "jumped in" to the MS gang several years before, and his size helped forge his reputation. He was also very good-looking. Girls from all backgrounds were in love with him and swooned over his every word. When Danger hung out in the Ceiba, girls were sure to be there. Even though the girls all liked Danger, the other gang members were able to flirt and sometimes secure dates from the ones Danger rejected. Because of this, the idea of his leaving the gang was opposed with a lot of pressure.

When I saw Danger again, he acted like he'd never met me. He had his friends introduce me to him to keep up the appearance. I asked him how he was doing. He said things were looking up, and his studies were excellent. After that, I kept up with Danger through his mom and siblings. His mom had told me before that Antonio and his father had had many fights over the gang situation. She said Antonio, out of all her kids, was most like her husband. It caused stress in the home when he and Antonio didn't see eye to eye.

The last time I spoke to his mom, she told me Antonio was calming down and was more attentive to his studies and his family. He was starting to distance himself little by little from his homeboys. She said his father and he were getting along, and Antonio was even taking an interest in his father's business. All the children were happy to have peace.

Several months later, one day after classes, Antonio's younger brother Angel arrived at my door. Angel started to cry and pleaded with me to come with him. He said his father had died. I asked if we were going to his house, and through the sobs, he said yes.

I rushed to grab some money and my Bible, and when I came back to the gate, small Angel was trying to compose himself. I hurt for him. He was eleven, the same age I had been when my dad had died. I wondered how each of the children would deal with their father's death. Most of all, I worried over Antonio's reaction. Would he be angry again? Would he seek comfort in his old habits? Would he start hanging out in the Ceiba again with his homeboys? Things had just settled down. Angel and I quickly wound around the road and reached his house. Gusano, one of my bus driver friends, was there. He smiled contently.

Angel raced up the steps to his home. Gusano walked with me and explained what had happened. He said his brother-in-law had had a massive coronary. The ambulance had not arrived in time, and he had died, leaving behind his wife and seven children.

I entered the house and received a cup of juice. The casket took center stage. Encircling it, people wept and held each other. I just sat down on one of the chairs that was lined up in front of the casket for visitors to sit and view the body. Gusano sat with me, and we talked of other things. He told me Giselle, the only daughter, was having the hardest time of all the children. She had been her father's favorite, and he had adored her. She was in my second-grade class, and I liked her very much. She had a ready smile and a sweet spirit. My heart broke for her that so young she had lost someone so important.

The youngest child, Natan, stood silently by the casket. He kept touching his father's hair. His round belly stuck out, and his eyes were wide and sad. He had to stretch up on his tiptoes to see his dad. He reminded me of my little sister who had done the same thing at my father's funeral. It was very touching.

I sought out and found Giselle sitting in a separate room, crying silently. She refused to look at me. I put my arm around her and told her it was okay to cry. I asked her to tell me about her dad. She smiled through the tears and told me how much she loved him. I told her he had loved her too and that he was in heaven and watching her now, making sure she was okay.

When I told her about my father, she looked up at me. She asked how old I had been. We talked about my feelings and how I had dealt with his death. I told her she could talk to her father still. She wondered if our fathers were talking as we were talking. I told her they just might be. She liked that. I decided to leave her alone, so she could think. She thanked me, grabbed my neck, and hugged me for a long time.

I went back to Gusano. As we talked, Antonio slowly walked into the house. He was followed by a large group of students from his school. Looking into the casket, he touched his father's hand. When he saw me, he came over and sat by me. I extended my sympathies. He thanked me and looked at the coffin as he talked. "More than anything, I am glad that my dad got to see me get out of the gang." He smiled and so did I. I told him I was sure it had brought his whole family great joy when he had left the gang.

Antonio continued his studies. He helps his mother and younger siblings with money as much as he is able. He is a strong son, full of love and respect. He is walking with God. He is one of the true survivors. He has walked both sides and chosen wisely. His quick smile and gentle spirit belie that he ever was Danger.

Chapter 17

"Look, Kylla, this guy … he's not really part of the gang … I mean, he's a gang member, but we don't like him that much. He needs a lot of help. I told him about the gang rehabilitation house, and he wants to go with you. Can you talk to him?"

"Of course, Gato. Thanks."

"No problem, you know how it is. His name is Garobo."

He was crouched under the big tree that stood in the Ceiba. His clothes were tattered and dirty. He hung his head and looked bewildered. He wanted out of the gang and into a new life.

I called out his tag name, Garobo, and he turned around. He smiled and jumped off the ledge where he had stooped and shook hands with Samuel and me. We asked him some basic questions. He didn't have a home. He and his father were enemies, and Garobo had left home during their last fight. He had an alcohol problem more than anything else. He stole to buy the liquor for a couple of quarters a pint. He was tired of his life.

"Look at me! My clothes are filthy; I'm hungry, cold, and unhappy. What kind of a life is this? I want to change my life. Can you help me?"

We told him we could help him, but that it would require much of him as well. He said he'd heard about

God being able to help him change his life. He asked how he could "get" God. We told him, and he prayed with us for salvation. After the "amen," when he lifted his face, he wiped away the tears of joy and smiled brightly.

We asked if he had everything he needed to go and live in the rehab home. He held up a small plastic bag with an extra pair of pants and said it was all he had. We flagged down a bus and headed off to Mejicanos.

Garobo, whose real name was Rafael Martin, thrived in the rehab home. He had lacked family structure all his life, and the routine and discipline of the home helped fill up the neediness of his heart. However, he had a hard time making friends. Because he was so desperate for acceptance and love, he tried too hard, and it made the other gang members uncomfortable. For example, he interrupted others' conversations to tell a story or joke that was out of place. The gang members would look at him strangely and continue their own conversation, excluding Garobo from further entry. He shared too much of his anger and bitterness with strangers, leaving them feeling uncomfortable and wanting to flee from his presence. He lacked the social skills necessary for an easy transition.

Rafael Martin had originally joined the gang because of his addiction. But he had been an outsider, even in the clique. The other gang members had laughed at him and were standoffish. Rafael Martin had internalized the rejection and drunk even more, trying desperately to fit into the group. The more he had tried, the more he had been shunned. His efforts had been annoying at best, isolating at worst.

So it was at the home. The leaders of the home tried to compensate for his lack of friends. They gave him responsibilities and privileges. They teamed up with him when a partner activity arose. They did their best. Rafael Martin welcomed their attention but became overly dependent on them. He wore them out with his constant need to hang out and talk.

When I came to the home to visit, Rafael monopolized my time. He wanted to know everything about the gang members he'd left behind in Santo Tomas. He always sent messages to them through me. Half of the time when I delivered the messages, the recipients didn't know who'd sent them. I felt bad for Rafael Martin. I discovered that often times, the ones who are crying out for help the most are ignored because it's exhausting to help them.

I tried to do special things for Rafael Martin. I wanted him to feel loved. I wanted him to know God's love. Rafael soaked it up. He began calling me Mom—his spiritual mom. He called me once a week during the hour of phone privilege to talk to me and ask how I was doing.

He was sent out of the home many months later to begin his transition back into "real life." He was one of the few who wasn't anxious about his freedom being taken away by living in the home. He had stayed as long as he was allowed.

When he got out, he went to live in a pastor's home. He was given a job at a cheese factory and started a new life, but he had a problem on the job. When Rafael Martin's feelings were hurt, he flew into a rage and wanted to exact revenge on the offending person. His boss had yelled at him for messing up an order, and Rafael's hurt morphed into anger. He quit his job in a fury and went on a drinking binge.

I got a phone call from Rafael that same night. He was crying and asking me to pray for him, help him, come and see him, and I reassured him I would. Gently, I told him he needed to apologize to his boss. He refused. He then started telling me about his father and the hate he felt. I told him God wanted him to love and forgive. He told me he couldn't. We talked of other things.

I saw Rafael that weekend, and his spirits were high. The pastor with whom he lived had called in some favors and arranged for Rafael to start work at a delivery service. Rafael had to start immediately, which excited him, although he was still anxious about being hurt. I gave him a pep talk and told him how everyone makes mistakes at work. I encouraged him to let the small things go and to pray about everything else. He nodded his head in agreement and promised to try.

Rafael Martin and I talked off and on for the last year I was in El Salvador. We spent hours discussing his father and the need to forgive. I knew there was some deep pain in Rafael Martin's heart over his dad, because he couldn't keep his father out of a conversation.

Once he determined to make his change, Rafael continued to thrive. Of course he had ups and downs;

however, he hung on tenaciously. He needed someone believing in him, and he found support in the church more than anywhere else. He wanted to please and be pleasing. Most of all, he wanted to be loved.

In one of the last conversations we shared, Rafael told me he had gone to see his father. He had talked to his dad and forgiven him for what he had done and had asked for forgiveness for his own hateful actions of retaliation. His father had listened and accepted the apology but hadn't offered one back. Rafael was disappointed about that. I congratulated Rafael on his maturity and told him he had done the right thing whether his father recognized it or not. I told him how proud I was of him. Rafael must have beamed on the other end of the line. I could hear the smile in his voice as he thanked me for my words.

He was still working and attending church when I left. I think of him often and hope he's continued to make right choices. I miss the phone calls in the middle of the night, when I'd pick up the receiver and hear the sweet voice of a champion say, "Hello, Mother. It's me, Rafael Martin."

Chapter 18

The market was filled with the same swarm of people day in and day out. Pungent odors assaulted the senses as people wove their way through the stalls and undulating mass of humanity. Cumbia and salsa music blared from stores and buses. Exhaust blinded the eyes and choked the throat as individuals, either in clusters or solitary, crossed the street.

Women laden with food baskets carried atop their heads, yelled to the passersby, "Guineos ... dos a cólon. Sopa de patas ... cinco pesos. Pupusas de frijol ... a dos."[37] Men pushed past the sellers, rushing to their jobs of loading and carrying. Children stood close to their mothers until they spotted one another and ran off to play.

The voices of barterers sounded shrilly over the rumble of buses. Cobradores hung out of the buses and petitioned the crowds to board. Half-starved dogs fought each other for littered food in the dirty streets.

Gang members, who charged "rent" to the organized vendors, looked tough huddling in groups of three and four. Their tattoos were prominently displayed on their bronzed arms and faces. Crazed gluesniffers staggered through the booths, barely missing the buses that plowed ahead with no regard for human life.

A man in a suit, holding a Bible, cast out demons from a filthy man with dreadlocks who writhed on the ground. Formed in a semicircle, a group of people stared at a woman who had been mugged and was lying face down in the road. They clucked sympathetically. No one did anything else.

Siblings fended for themselves while their moms sold food or talked to friends. A two-year-old shared an apple crate with her infant sister. Both were dirty and silent. They wouldn't have been heard in the midst of the activity. Instinctively, they knew.

Young girls who had ceased to dream a long time before sold shampoo, oil, or food in the market. They would not go to school. They would never live outside the market. It was their destiny, and they accepted it without a fight.

Thieves and prostitutes maneuvered their way past the vendors, making passes or stealing a banana or two. They were someone's relatives, and therefore, not a threat. They sat and chatted with their friends and lovers. It was a family.

Drug dealers stood on corners and looked the part. Seedy and with darting eyes, they counted out money and passed small bags back and forth. The local police patrolled the market; seeing nothing, hearing nothing, doing nothing.

A random tourist who happened upon the market was tagged and robbed. It was a smooth operation; the victim didn't even know his pockets had been lightened. Gringos were insulted and, at the same time, pressured to buy. The vendors had family in the U.S.

They knew how their relatives were treated. They paid it back in spades to those who dared walk into their territory.

Older women, veterans of the market, pulled their chairs close together and caught up on the latest news and gossip. They sat, relaxed, not trying to sell. They didn't see the point of yelling. They had a clientele for their wares. They were established.

Younger women smiled at the cops and gangsters. They wanted the security of a man. A cop would be better, but they covered their bases. The gangsters and cops played the game and had many women in the market.

There were pockets of peace. There were vendors who had large stalls, complete with televisions, radios, and comfortable chairs. Their families sat, pleasant to all who passed by, and carried on a normal life in the market. They sold and smiled, happy and content with their lives.

Students arrived in the afternoons after school to help their parents in these stalls. They greeted their extended families as they ran past the countless women and men sitting and selling. They had dreams and were free to be.

I was on my way to the bank to cash a check but had decided to walk through the market to buy a baseball cap. I had been challenged by some of the bus drivers to bargain down the price. They wouldn't tell me how much I should pay, only instructing me to force the price as low as possible. I ended up spending a mere thirty cólones, about four dollars, on my hat. I was extremely proud of myself for my excellent bartering skills. I couldn't wait to gloat to the bus drivers.

I wound around the streets until I arrived in Plaza Morazon, an MS-controlled downtown park. It was there that I needed to flag down a number 30 bus to get to my bank. I stood on the sidewalk, chuckling to myself about what I could say to the bus drivers to put them in their places since they had joked with each other about how badly I would be cheated, when I saw her.

She danced around the couples that stood near me in Plaza Morazon waiting for the bus. Her pants were baggy and too short for her. Her white shirt was stained and un-tucked. She had cropped hair and wore no make-up. She was a little strange.

She circled around the females, sizing them up, and then hitting them on the arm, asking for money. Each young woman she approached took a step back, tried to ignore her, and clutched her purse a little tighter.

One of the women she hit up for money showed too much fear. The crazy lady saw her chance and harassed the woman until she had extracted the desired cólon. She then sidled up to her next victim. Unfortunately for the ragged woman, her new prey had a boyfriend, and he prevented her from receiving anything.

I'd been watching this whole scene from about five yards away. I giggled because of the comical way the woman danced around her victims. She heard me snicker and approached. She began her trademark circling, like a vulture around its meal. When she came around in front of me, she stopped. Her eyes took in my whole body, starting at my feet and working their way up. Her head was arched back, her mouth agape, and her eyes on my eyes at the end of the tour. My being a good ten inches taller, as well as far larger than her, seemed to do the trick. She shook her head and moved away.

As if on impulse, she ran to the curb where some buses were parked and threw her arms wide open. She began to yell and whistle, which attracted some attention from passengers on the bus. Shaking her whole body, she performed a sort of shimmy dance. People laughed, not with her, but at her. She hooted too, but after a moment, she realized the laughter was more jeering than friendly. She looked around, shot each woman on the corner a nasty look, and re-approached me.

I stood looking down at her. She circled me and then stood by my side. As people made their way through the busy park, she insulted them and jerked her head toward me. It made it appear as if we were partners, friends, consorts in these games of hers. The people she insulted would look to me. I'd smile apologetically, and they'd continue on their way.

I glanced at her, and she stared right back. I nonchalantly asked if she'd like something to drink. She calmly stated she'd like an orange juice. After I bought the juice, she looked intently at me for a long time before speaking.

"Why'd you buy me a juice?"

"It looked like you needed something. Was I right?"

"I need a friend."

I introduced myself and ventured that we could be juice buddies. She laughed and nodded her head vigorously in agreement. I gave her a hug and told her I'd see her later. She smiled and waved goodbye as I boarded my bus.

Chapter 19

One hot Salvadoran morning, I went to catch the bus into town so I could attend church. Gato wasn't there, and the bus drivers told me there had been a fight. Some 18th Street gang members had encountered him and other Salvatrucha members downtown the night before. They had flashed their signs, and it had begun. My stomach tightened as I asked how Gato was. They explained to me he had been slashed across the forehead with a machete.

Without waiting to hear any more, I dashed across the street to his house and pushed myself in through the rusted door. His mom met me at the gate and led me through the house and into Gato's bedroom. His head was bandaged, like a mummy, with huge white gauze wrapped around his head several times, and he was in severe pain. Crossing the dirt floor and sitting on the edge of the mattress, I listened as he recounted what had happened.

He and some homeboys had gone to a dance down across from the downtown bus stop. They were leaving to buy some drinks at a nearby bar when they saw a tough-looking group of ten 18th Street gang members. Recognizing one another as rival gang members, the two groups started throwing gang signs and building up their bravado to engage the other side in a battle. The next thing he knew, they were all fighting. One of Gato's homeboys had a knife and stabbed someone, and an 18th Streeter pulled out a machete and started swinging it violently, which was when Gato had been hit.

Gato finished the story and then peeled off the bandages to display the raw and bloody gash. Because the machete had a slight curve to it, the mark it left resembled a perfect Nike swoosh.

Gato had a propensity for wearing Nike hats, shirts, and shoes. At a distance, I could always tell it was him when a group of guys were hanging out together. So seeing the violent swoosh etched into his head made me laugh at the irony.

"At least now you don't have to buy anymore Nike baseball caps, Gato."

His other friends who were visiting laughed too, and Gato joined in, although it hurt his head to do so. Our humor was a cover for our concern and fears. I just looked at him and patted his outstretched leg. Suddenly, the seriousness of the moment dawned on me, and I felt a deep fear inside my heart for him.

I began to beg him, "Gato, you have to quit the gang. You have served in the gang for a long time now. You don't have to stay. It's stupid, and it's too dangerous. You could die, and you just have to leave it behind."

The pain he was feeling helped drive my point as the tears welled up in his eyes. I pleaded with him to listen to me and leave the gang. The fearful child trapped inside him heard me. I could see it in his eyes. When he looked at me like that, it was as if his eyes held out a little hope that life didn't really have to be as bad as it had been. His eyes locked on mine in a moment of silent pleading. I shook my head. "Gato, you just have to leave it."

When I spoke, the moment broke. His eyes changed from those of a sad little boy to ones of an angry youth. "I'm not going to leave my gang … Salvatrucha for life. What I need is revenge, nothing else."

I knew his speech, made through gritted teeth, was to preserve his dignity. To make himself feel strong, he had to pledge his need for blood. To forget how bad his life was, he had to cling to the life he had made for himself within the gang. He couldn't be weak. He wiped his tears away, and we changed the subject.

When the bandages came off a few weeks later, the Nike scar prominently displayed, Gato stepped out into the street again. His khakis were starched and ironed. His shirt displayed a big 13, and his hands twitched nervously through his memorized gang signs. He said he needed to be with his homies. They would figure out what to do.

There were a lot of people on both sides of the church, the ironic place where the Salvatrucha hung out. One afternoon, stepping off the bus and greeting Oso, Killer, and Good Boy, I asked if they'd seen Gato. Killer pointed across the street. Gato sat slumped over on the edge of the sidewalk, his hands repeating the routine of gang signs. Killer told me Gato was drunk.

We crossed the street to where Gato was, and I said hi. He responded by throwing up all over his shoes. His shirt was covered in vomit as well. Standing up, with tears streaming down his face, Gato began defending his mother's honor, which hadn't been attacked. He stumbled and fell on the pavement, and we picked him up.

That was when I noticed an older lady, sad and worn, pulling Gato into her lap. I recognized his mother from when I had visited Gato after his injury. She sat stoically on the little pavement stoop. It was obvious she had been through this before. She shifted her body weight and prepared herself for the long night ahead.

As Gato lay peacefully in his mother's lap, amid his vomit and the crowd, I leaned over to her and formally introduced myself. I told her I was going to try to get Gato home. She thanked me and said she hoped we could.

I flagged down one of the buses. I knew the driver and cobrador, so they got out and helped me lift Gato into the bus. His mother boarded after us, and we sped down the road. The other passengers moved closer to the windows because of the nauseating stench.

Arriving at Gato's house, we carried him inside and laid him down. Back outside, his mother thanked us graciously, even though we hadn't really done anything. She turned from us and entered her house. I went home full of sadness because I knew Gato was miserable, but I didn't know how to help him, how to reach him, or even if he wanted my help.

Chapter 20

Vendors lined the parks in San Salvador. They sold everything anyone would want. In Parque Libertad,[38] the vendors sat calmly under their makeshift umbrellas and tents, waiting for customers in need of water and candy. Eighteenth Street gang members bought water, juice, or a piece of gum, and talked to the vendors and their daughters. It was rare to visit the shops without having to acknowledge one or two gangsters, since they were an omnipresent reality.

I felt like God wanted me to sweep the park, literally. I didn't know why, and I still don't totally know. I just did it. Samuel and I started out one afternoon, armed with our newly purchased brooms, and began sweeping. The dialogue between the vendors and us went more or less like the following: "Hi, we were wondering if you had any trash we could throw away for you. We'd like to clean your booth up for you."

The response was accompanied by apprehensive looks and questions: "Why are you doing this? What is your problem?"

We smiled and said, "Jesus loves you and wants you to have a great day."

The chemistry was wonderful right from the start. The vendors thought we were insane, the gang members mocked us, and we sweated and cleaned. We swept every week, and every week, the conversations were merely variations of the original theme.

After a few months of sweeping, the vendors began to anticipate our arrival. The gang members stopped hassling us, and we were able to engage in intelligent banter with the park's populace. One vendor in particular seemed to need our company.

She had a son named Mateo. She had named him that for her faith. As a poor, single mother, she explained that she'd raised him the best she could. At twenty, he had left home and become a cocaine addict. She didn't know what to do. She asked us to pray for her because her prayers weren't working, and she wanted someone else to help her.

We started to pray for all the vendors. We asked them what their requests were, and we prayed. We prayed for Mateo to return home, to get the help he needed, and to find God. We prayed for another vendor's sons who needed jobs. We prayed for people's health and finances. We swept and prayed.

One week as we swept, the vendors started to tell us of the changes in their lives. The vendor who had been worried about her sons' employment told us they had both received jobs. Health was improving in some lives, finances in others. Some people had no changes. But we were very happy and excited as we rounded the corner of the park.

"Mateo is home now!" she shouted the good news excitedly and smiled. She hugged us tightly and thanked us profusely for praying. Later that year she brought Mateo to the park to meet us. We took a picture, and whenever I look at it, I smile.

In sweeping the park, Samuel and I gained entry into the 18th Street clique that ruled the area. The day Gato had been slashed with a machete, I visited the park to find the gang member who had been stabbed by Gato's clique. His story had been identical to Gato's, save for the fact that instead of the Salvatrucha being outnumbered, his version stated that the 18th Street was heavily outmanned.

"Who got stabbed?"

"Loquito, the guy over there."

I walked over to where Loquito had been regaling his homeboys with war stories from the fight he had just survived, shook his hand, and asked him if he was all right. He lifted his shirt and showed me the stab wound. It wasn't too deep, but blood had covered the white bandage, which made it very dramatic. When I gasped a little, he chuckled.

"It was nothing, Gringa. But we macheted this asshole so good that he'll never forget."

All of the gangsters had laughed and flashed the 18th Street sign, cursing Gato, hoping he would die, mocking what he must look like now.

"That guy's going to be so ugly … he was ugly before, but now, people are going to be scared to look at him."

My stomach tightened, and I wanted to scream at them to shut up. They didn't know Gato. I was furious at their insults, but I knew the Salvatrucha clique was having a good laugh about Loquito's stab wound as well.

The insanity of the gangs struck me in that moment. Loquito and Gato could have been friends had it not been for the self-inflicted tattoos and gang protocol. They had similar backgrounds, a shared culture, and fun personalities. But once the numbers 13 and 18 dominated their thinking, they were more comfortable killing each other and reveling in it than extending their circle of friends.

Chapter 21

I had gone to buy pupusas from the lady whose boy-friend hit her. I felt bad for her and wanted her to have enough money to leave him. I wasn't naïve though; I knew she wouldn't leave. She would be the one left when he decided she wasn't good enough anymore.

It was fairly early when I got there. I ordered my pupusas and sat at the broken table waiting for her to cook them. At the table with me was an older man who had been drinking.

When he looked up from his beer, he struck up a conversation with me. He asked my name and then introduced himself. His name was Don Juan, which I thought was funny, but I stifled a laugh. He informed me he knew who I was—"the coffee girl." He commented on my work with the gang members and nodded his approval. Then he whispered that I looked like a lady he had known earlier in his life. With that last sentence, he whimpered and began to cry.

Startled by the unexpectedness of the crying, I asked him what was wrong. He wiped his eyes and told me the story of a nun who had lived in El Salvador during the war. He said she had been young and a good person like me. She had loved the people and helped them when they needed it. He said she had been a missionary and very kind. Then the tears overtook him, and he cried again.

The lady making pupusas looked at me and shook her head compassionately. I patted the man on the back, and his large body heaved a long sigh. He told me I reminded him of the nun. He said we would have been friends. Don Juan had met her when she had helped the people in his town get needed supplies. He didn't know me, but he said he felt like he did.

He began sobbing again. Between the cries, he screamed that she had been raped and killed by soldiers here. He was intermittently angry and sad. He kept repeating that they had raped a nun—four of them. How could they rape and kill nuns? How could they do that to ladies who had come to help the people? How could they rape the sisters?

I knew what he was talking about, and the case had yet to be tried. For a crime committed so many years ago, it was inexcusable. He touched my face with his large, calloused hand. He stammered that I looked like her; and whether I did or not didn't matter; he believed it in that moment. He told me to be careful and watch out for the soldiers. I assured him that I would be okay, that I would avoid the soldiers and he shouldn't worry. He nodded his approval.

I paid for my pupusas and thanked the lady for making them so well. I waved goodbye to both her and the inconsolable man. He kept crying and yelling after me, "Be careful. Be careful with the soldiers."

I wanted to tell him the war was over and the military wasn't patrolling the streets, but I thought better of it. He seemed frozen in time, drinking his beer, and remembering the horrors he must have seen in his lifetime. That night it seemed as if the war would never stop raging.

When I arrived home, sobered by Don Juan's speech, the phone rang. There'd been a scuffle at Parque Libertad. The cops had been doing a routine search of the gang members, lining them up against the wall and searching them. It was more a show of force than anything meaningful. The gang members always knew when the cops were coming and ditched their weapons.

The details provided in the call were sketchy at best. For whatever reason, Caballo had moved during the search. A cop had thought he was bolting and shot. Luckily, the bullet had gone through him at an angle, entering the left side of his stomach and exiting the right side. He would live, but it put him out of commission for a few weeks.

I went to the park the following day and talked to Prima. She was a vendor in the park who sympathized with 18th Street and was indeed a member's cousin, hence the nickname. She was rough-talking and hard-working. Her voice was gravelly from lack of sleep and overuse. She sold candy, mints, gum, and water in her little stand by the street. Her daughter and grandson worked with her.

I asked her to tell me what had happened. She vividly described how the rookie cop had haphazardly fired his gun. She was angry and excited, glad she was being asked to give an account of the events. I told her I wanted to go and visit Caballo. She stared at me warily in silence and muttered something under her breath, but then agreed to meet me at her candy stand the following day and accompany me to Caballo's house.

I arrived at her stand at 2:00 p.m. and waited because Prima wasn't there. Her daughter laughed at me and said she was surprised I'd shown up. They didn't think I would really visit Caballo. Eighteenth Street believed me to be an MS sympathizer because I lived in Santo Tomas and hung out with the guys on the 21 bus line. All my attempts to befriend 18th Street gang members were hindered by that fact. I had also been threatened by a gang member in the MS who thought I was sympathetic to 18th Street.

He had grabbed my arm and told me in English that he needed to tell me something. His name was Batman, and he was an ex-gang member from MS. He hadn't left the gang because of some moral change; rather, he had connections with the organized crime groups and had paid his dues to the gang. He was OG, original gangster,[39] having jumped into the gang in Los Angeles, and faced no repercussions for leaving his clique.

We had met because he lived in my town and was a bus driver. He whispered to me, "I saw you in the park with 18th Street. What were you doing there?"

I told him I had been talking to 18th Street members, just as I took coffee to the bus drivers, because I felt like God was telling me to do it. He shook his head impatiently and pressed my arm a little tighter. "You better be careful what you do. You can't be on both sides. Something can happen to you. You gonna start taking coffee to 18, too?"

I laughed and told him that I swept the park, and coffee was not on the agenda. His eyes narrowed. "Look, I'm not going to hurt you. I heard other people talking. You just better be careful. You need to choose sides."

I defiantly looked him in the eyes and demanded to know who was talking. He refused to tell me. I then informed him that I was on neither side; I was part of God's gang, and the angels were my homeboys. Annoyed, he yelled that I was stupid. I smiled calmly and asked for him to let me go. He released my arm, and as he walked away, he shouted over his shoulder, "Don't tell me I didn't warn you."

So I understood that it wasn't easy for either side of the gang world to appreciate my position, but I was determined to treat everyone the same no matter what number was burned into their flesh.

Prima showed up at 3:00 p.m. She didn't apologize for being an hour late. Her eyebrows rose, and a smile crept onto her face. She was as surprised as her daughter that I was there. I asked if she was ready to take me to Caballo. She nodded, and we crossed the park to hail the bus.

Once seated, I realized I'd brought nothing to give Caballo as a get-well gift. Luckily, a thin, exhausted-looking man boarded the bus and slowly made his way up and down the crowded aisle shouting, "Mangoes for sixty cents." I purchased a bag. Everyone liked mangoes, so I was glad they were available. Prima and I tried to have a conversation on the bus, but she knew so many people, she ended up talking to all of them instead. I sat on the old school bus that had been converted into El Salvador's public transportation and bounced along the pot-holed road, without having the comfort of good shocks to cushion the jolts, and looked out the window. I had no idea where I was going.

Thirty minutes later, Prima hit my leg and motioned for me to stand up and shove my way to the back of the bus. I knew we must be close to our stop. We got off at a rather barren place; there weren't a lot of houses or anything where we were. She grabbed my arm and pulled me, running, across the highway. We walked up a dirt embankment, and from nowhere, a small house emerged on our right. We climbed the cement steps and knocked on the door.

A very tired-looking young woman answered the door. She had a baby in her arms, which couldn't have been more than a few weeks old. She smiled at Prima and looked at me questioningly. I introduced myself and told her I'd like to see Caballo. She opened the door wider, and we entered the house.

Caballo was lying on a green cot covered with mosquito netting. His stomach was wrapped with white gauze. He struggled to sit up when he saw us. There were two children playing in a corner of the house. It was a nice one-room house, large enough to make distinctions between each area: bedroom, playroom, kitchen, etc. The kids ignored us and continued playing.

Caballo's wife moved to his side and handed him the baby. He gingerly held his son to his chest. It was always strange to me when I saw the tenderness gang members displayed for their children or for friends. It seemed like a contradiction, yet I knew they were just like me, save for the gangs they loved.

I gave him the mangoes, and he thanked me. We made small talk. He told me about his wound and his family. Prima was yelling over our lackluster conversation to Caballo's wife about how nice the house was. She liked the breeze that continually flowed. She liked how light everything was. She wanted to move in with them. Caballo and his wife chuckled and avoided saying anything.

It was a fairly uneventful visit. Caballo was shocked I was there. He didn't know what to say, and neither did I. I prayed for him and told him I hoped to see him again soon. His wife sighed. She knew he would be back in the park soon enough. He never learned, and she was worn down.

Prima and I left, and she told me that Caballo's wife wanted to leave him and have a life that wasn't interrupted by gunshot wounds, police visits, and homeboys. We stood on the side of the road, waiting for a bus to take us into San Salvador. A bus we hadn't flagged down pulled over to the side of the road, and the driver and cobrador began cat-calling me.

Prima laughed and pushed me forward. She found it amusing that these men were harassing me. I ducked my head and tried to back away behind Prima. The packed bus had been stopped for over two minutes, while the bus driver with his black beret and dark sunglasses leaned over the passengers in the front seat to tell me how beautiful I was. Prima and I engaged in a dance of me backing up behind her, and her dodging to the right or left to leave me no hiding place. After about five minutes of this ridiculous game, the passengers' complaints of wanting to reach their destination and not waste time on me had reached a crescendo, and the driver and cobrador pulled away, blowing kisses at me and swearing they would return.

Prima told me I shouldn't be embarrassed, that I should dress better and flirt more; with blonde hair and blue eyes, I had potential. I thanked her and insisted in my most irritated tone that I wasn't in need of a boyfriend. She laughed so hard at me, she snorted. I was not amused.

The bus ride back to the park seemed to last forever. When we arrived, Prima was immediately surrounded by gang members seeking information on how Caballo was doing. She explained that he was well and, glancing at me through the corner of her eyes, informed the gang members I'd gone with her. Their conversation stopped as several of them looked at me, nodding their heads in approval. The looks were given to me with a new and hard-earned respect. A few of them even came over and shook my hand.

A week later I saw Caballo. He halted a conversation he was having with fellow 18th Street members and sauntered over to Prima's stand where I was buying water and shook my hand, asking how I was. I smiled, telling him I was well, and asked if the pain had gone away. He lifted his shirt and showed me the scar. He said he was okay. He was ready to begin his crazy life again; not even a bullet could stop him.

Chapter 22

Darkness cloaked the town. The silence was thick, save for the occasional bus roaring down the main road. It was a cool night, perhaps eighty degrees, and I put on a sweater that I carried in my bag. Having become well acclimated to Santiago Texacuango weather, eighty degrees with a breeze sent a chill down my spine.

My bus let me off at the phone booth in my town, and I inhaled deeply. The scent of mangoes wafted through the sweet air. It was a good night. I started walking home.

I couldn't see anything really. The businesses had closed for the night, there were no lights, and I had to stare down at my feet to make out my next steps. A shrill whistle punctuated the silent night. I whipped around to look, but blackness stared back at me.

The whistle sounded again. I knew it was Gato's. Stopping, I called out his name, hoping the air would bring an answer back to me. "Come here," he yelled. I turned around and made my way toward his voice, laughing when I bumped into him. He had come half-way to meet me, and since I had been staring at my feet, I hadn't seen his.

"You are such a vaga," he laughed. Vaga was my nickname. It meant vagabond. The bus drivers joked about how much I stayed out in the streets, never at home. I told Gato I'd been in Mejicanos, and he asked how the boys were there. He didn't know them, but since they were members of the MS, he acted interested. I told him they were fine.

We strolled back over to the stoop he'd been occupying with two of his friends. They were both gang members, recent inductees. They knew me by reputation, nothing more. After I said hi to them, they continued their conversation, as Gato talked to me.

He brought up our friend Killer and how he had left the gang, come back, and left again … the never-ending cycle. He wanted to know why Killer couldn't make up his mind. I explained about Killer fighting a spiritual battle. He didn't have the supports he needed around him to make a clean break, and besides, leaving a gang was a slow process anyway.

Gato nodded his head. He picked up a twig and began making circles in the dirt we sat on. We sat in silence for a while, and then he said in a whisper that he wasn't going to be a preacher. He didn't want to preach. He didn't want to go to seminary, and he didn't want to teach about God.

Stunned by his pronouncement, I thought, *I have never told him he needed to be a preacher.* I wondered who had. I assured him he wasn't tied to any one occupation and that he didn't have to be a preacher at all. He shook his head, agitated, and told me everyone getting out of the gang went to seminary.

I explained to Gato that God doesn't call everyone to preach. I told him there were so many jobs to be done, and they weren't even all in ministry. He stared up at me, interested in what I was saying. I kept going, listing a number of occupations, including teacher, bus driver, pilot, and plumber. He could do anything he wanted to do.

He shook his head and insisted he was destined for a life in the gang. He couldn't get out, and there was no job waiting for him. He said only rich people have the opportunity to change their fate. I told him several stories about people who had gone from poverty to success.

As I spoke, I noticed a small glimmer of hope appear in his eyes—the same look I had seen in his eyes before when he had thought about his life outside the gang. He asked how they had done it. I told him he had to study and work hard. He needed to leave the gang in order to devote time to his dream. I realized at the same time Gato did that the other guys had stopped talking and were listening to our conversation. As if on cue, Gato's eyes hardened, and he looked toward the other gangsters and back at me and said, "Well, I'm going to die in my gang … Trucha for life."

The other gangsters chuckled and gave high-fives to Gato. I ignored their display, maintained my eye contact with Gato, and informed him that his mentality was cowardly. Offended and embarrassed, he asked me how he could be a coward when he would throw up gang signs in 18th Street territory and had taken many hits as a gang member.

I told him he, along with the others, was hiding behind the tattoos and attitudes because he was scared of failing at other things. A truly courageous man would face the future with a plan, would fail and pick himself up, instead of running to the gang and hiding out. I told him he was scared to try, so he used the excuse of not being able to leave the gang. He needed to be strong, not in some fleeting, bravado way, but rather in a lasting, effective way. I kept going, giving examples, talking about courage and strength. I don't know how long I talked.

When I stopped, there was a heavy silence between us. The other gang members said goodbye and left disgustedly. Gato sat staring at the ground. In a whisper, he asked, "Do you really think I'm a coward?" His voice was small, and it made me uncomfortable. I lifted his face to mine. I told him I thought he had courage, but he wasn't using it. I urged him to use it.

We sat in silence for a time. I was shaking a bit as the seriousness of our conversation dawned on me. Gato was quiet, crouched on the ground next to me. The darkness kept us in its arms. We sat alone, engulfed in our thoughts, wishing life were different and wanting so desperately to understand one another more. I don't remember how long we stayed there in silence, Gato staring at the ground, and me watching him.

"Gato, you have to know I love you. I want to see you living a different kind of life. You're a leader. You see how people look up to you. You have got to start using this gift for good. Look, I'm sorry if I hurt you with what I said."

He looked up at me and held my gaze. "It's okay, Vaga. I know you just want to help me." He poked me with the stick and laughed. "Hey, remember when you went swimming in that cesspool over there?" And he pointed over to the sewer-filled ditch that was under construction by the bus depot. I had slipped and fallen into the filthy cesspool a few months back, when had I tried to squeeze past a bus to get to the diner.

"Ah, yeah, how could I forget such a thing? That water was so disgusting. I almost threw up. And I was so completely wet, and my dress was stuck to me so I couldn't even walk."

"It was so funny, Kylla. We all call that pit your swimming pool now."

"That's great … and the next time I go swimming, I'll be sure to invite you."

"Hell no! I'm not swimming there." We both laughed at the thought of it. We said our goodnights and went to our houses to sleep. It had been a really good night.

Chapter 23

On my way downtown, I sat in the front seat of Panda's bus, talking with him as he angled the bus through narrow streets and heinous traffic. Gato was his cobrador, and after Gato finished collecting bus fare, he leaned over the back of our seat and joined our conversation.

"Man, Kylla is going to Parque Libertad again today."

Gato rolled his eyes as he told Panda I was on my way to visit 18th Street gang members.

"Kylla, you shouldn't hang out with them. They'll kill you. They aren't like the kids in the Ceiba. They're for real crazy."

Offended, Gato yelled, "Hey, we are crazy too man; pocos pero locos."[40]

Panda jerked the van over to the side of the road when he saw a young girl's hand waving. Gato fluidly moved from where he was leaning over to the bus door and pulled it open, helping the girl into the bus and collecting her fare. He returned to his position between us.

"She's hot, man, don't you think?"

Gato licked his lips and asked me what I thought of the girl. He always asked me about the girls he flirted with. Did I think they were pretty? Did I think they looked good together? He always had a new girl, so they became a blur to me.

"Gato, how many girlfriends do you have?" I asked him.

"Thousands, Kylla, thousands."

We were approaching Parque Libertad, so I said my goodbyes and grabbed my bag. Gato crossed himself as he debarked and opened the door for me to step off the bus. It was dangerous for a gang member to be in enemy territory, even if he was working. As soon as my feet touched down, I turned around to wave at Panda and Gato, but the bus was already rattling down the road. I went and bought lemonade.

Bugs and Ghost, two 18th Street gang members, were supposed to come over to Samuel's house with me to watch movies and eat junk food. They were best friends and two of the toughest gang girls I'd met. A mutual friend had orchestrated this meeting, and I was nervous, but anxious to get to know them.

Ghost was pregnant again. She had lost so many babies during fights that it had become a joke. Her eyebrows were shaved and new ones painted on with eyeliner. The arched brows and dark eye makeup were supposed to make her look tough, and along with the tattoos across her chin and arms, they did. She had held a knife to my neck the first time we met. I had walked right into an 18th Street meeting, which, in retrospect, had been stupid. I knew the leader, Maniaco, and so had been allowed to live.

Bugs was Maniaco's girlfriend. She was tough, too. After she had sustained injuries in a drive-by grenade attack, she had limped painfully back into the park to show her loyalty. Her eyebrows were of the eyeliner brand as well. Her tattoos were on hands and body; her face remained pure. The girls should have been at the park at 3:00 p.m. but weren't.

Cactus wandered over and sat by me on the dividing wall. He told me stories between cigarettes and made me laugh. He assured me the girls should be there soon enough. Cactus flashed the Salvatrucha hand signs to male passersby. They shook their heads and hurried to their destinations. It was 18th Street territory, and everyone knew it.

I asked Cactus why he flashed the enemy gang sign. He explained to me that he was seeking information about the Salvatrucha. I figured he didn't get many takers since the park was tagged with a huge 18. He whispered in my ear that I'd be surprised.

A few more guys rushed by, shrugged off Cactus's hand signs, and left. A young couple strolled past, and Cactus grinned and flashed the hand sign. The boy turned around and flashed back the MS for Mara Salvatrucha. Cactus leapt from the wall and shook the boy's hand with the MS handshake. They began talking. It was a lively conversation, punctuated by laughter. It appeared they were friends so I thought the whole episode was a joke. Cactus continued to extract vital information about the MS clique, leaders, and location from the boy.

The boy was still laughing when Cactus stiffened, threw down his cigarette, and flashed 18th Street's sign in the boy's face. The boy tried to run, and his girlfriend burst into tears. Cactus yelled, "Eighteen!" and ten members of 18th Street descended upon the boy, indelibly imprinting on his mind that he was in 18th Street territory, and he didn't belong.

The police, who were stationed in the park, heard the yells, and came running from their booth. Eighteenth Street scattered. The boy picked himself up and limped away, bloody and embarrassed. His weeping girlfriend offered him help that his battered ego forced him to refuse.

Cactus limped back to sit next to me ten minutes later, having twisted his ankle in the scuffle. He told me the boy had jumped into the gang only a week earlier. He was from the countryside and consequently didn't know which parks belonged to whom. Cactus expressed feeling bad about beating him but said he had had no choice. If anyone found out he hadn't beaten the boy, he could be put in green light[41] for disgracing the park and his own gang.

Cactus stared at me and chuckled. He took a drag from his cigarette and said, "And you thought nobody would fall for that. Welcome to my world."

Chapter 24

One of the cobradores on our bus line hanged himself. Too overwhelmed by his life and the lack of love he perceived in it, he wrote a love letter to his girlfriend, climbed up on a chair, and stepped off.

The mood was definitely solemn when I carried the coffee up to the bus drivers. They said Popo Loco had killed himself. I didn't understand what they were saying at first. I thought someone else had killed him, but I was wrong. Finally understanding what had happened, I started to cry. His tag was "Popo Loco," but I had known him as Giovanni. He was Salvatrucha, a cobrador on the bus line, and my friend.

He had been taller than me, which was rare among Salvadorans, and it was first thing I had noticed about him. He had also been very serious. He related well to the other drivers, even though he tended to avoid their backslapping humor. It was a challenge to get him to laugh, so it had become my goal.

The evenings I spent at the downtown bus depot were always lively. Typically, sixty of the hundred bus drivers from route 21 were there. We would laugh, talk, and share Cokes and pupusas. Often Giovanni would come and sit by me, greeting me with more respect than many of the others.

He always had some deep question to ask. He had been a thinker, despite his lack of formal education.

He would debate me on the United States' supremacy, the reasons behind El Salvador's civil war and subsequent violence, whether or not God was real, if God was going to destroy the United States, and where we would spend eternity. He would be finishing up his point when the bus would pull away, carrying him into the night.

Giovanni had a girlfriend whom he had loved. He had told me she was pregnant. He had been so excited, I didn't even have to try and make him smile. During the months, he had kept me updated on his girlfriend and soon-to-be son.

He had more questions than ever about God. He wanted to be a good father and teach his son the truth. He wanted to know where he himself stood. He had read and re-read the Bible I had given him months before. He kept questioning everything.

One evening, Giovanni came and sat next to me, putting his arm around me. He told me he loved me, and I told him the same. He couldn't stay long because his bus was leaving, so we said goodbye. It was the last time I saw him.

The drivers decorated their buses with black crepe paper, a final tribute to the strong and silent man. They took up a collection for his mother and little brother. A few even went to the house and cut down the poor, thin body of my friend and placed him in the casket they had brought.

They all had different theories as to why he'd done it. There was speculation that his girlfriend had a lover, and the baby she carried was the lover's and not

Giovanni's. Giovanni had discovered them together, and it had been too much for him, or so the story went. His suicide note, addressed to his girlfriend, spoke of love, nothing more.

I was devastated. He had been a true friend, yet I had no idea that he had been struggling with this huge question about his life. Gato arrived and came to tell me what I already knew. He asked if I would be going to the funeral, and I said I would. I asked him what time it would be, and he didn't know. One of the other bus drivers offered to call me and let me know in the morning.

I tried to comfort Gato by saying how sorry I was about Giovanni. They had been good friends. He hung his head and said he had to go. I knew he was fighting back tears. Reaching out and touching his arm, I asked, "Tomorrow, we'll go together, okay?" He nodded and turned away. I went back home to cry alone.

The next morning I waited by the phone. It didn't ring. I didn't know when or where the funeral was, so I felt like I needed to wait for directions. Finally, at 10:30 a.m., I went up to the bus depot to see if someone else knew where the funeral was. At the depot I asked, and they told me it was already over. I couldn't believe it. I suddenly felt sick.

I hung out, talking with the bus drivers about Giovanni, remembering him and the way he was. And then Gato's bus pulled up. He hurriedly walked over to me, and I could tell he was mad. His gait was almost like a charge.

"Where were you? It is so uncool that you didn't go. Was he your friend or not?" he demanded.

He was glaring at me, and the emotion in his voice heightened my own sense of guilt. I burst into tears. What Gato was saying, I was feeling. I felt like I had disrespected Giovanni by not going. I felt like I had let him down and sent a clear message to the other bus drivers that I really didn't care. So when Gato accused me of it, I completely understood.

As I stood there trying to get control of myself, Gato looked completely bewildered by my reaction to his words. His tone softened immediately. "Kylla, I'm sorry. Don't cry. I'm sorry. I'm just upset. Don't cry. Forgive me, okay?"

"I wanted to go. I was waiting for someone to call me and tell me when and where it was, but nobody called. I feel horrible, believe me."

He wiped my tears away. The other bus drivers moved away from us, and Gato and I were alone in the street.

"Gato, I'm so sorry."

"Shhh, Kylla, it's okay. He's in a better place now anyway."

He told me about the funeral and how so many people had turned out to pay their final respects. We talked about Giovanni and sadly laughed about times we had shared with him.

"I'm so sad, Gato. I don't understand why he'd kill himself. It doesn't make sense."

"I don't understand either, but he's at peace now."

He motioned to the driver of his bus that he would

be back. He told me he was going to walk me back to my house. We walked in silence, he with his hands stuffed deep in his pockets, and me with my arms crossed around myself. The grief we felt was tangible, and neither of us wanted to touch it. When I got to my door, we stood there for a brief moment. The earlier anger had subsided, and now sadness reigned.

"He was a good friend, you know?"

I nodded my head in agreement and turned around and went inside. From the doorway, I watched as Gato trudged back up the hill, his hands still helpless inside his pants pockets. I loved him so much. It became very clear to me in that moment that I never wanted to lose him. I didn't think I could deal with that. We had already lost enough.

Chapter 25

The scene was always the same in Parque Libertad, a surreal mix of woeful drama and dark comedy. Today I watched, not as someone merely crossing the street for a bus, but as a student preparing for an exam.

The park was a large cement plaza with the only grass in San Salvador growing in patches at its four corners. Outlining the park, vendors hawked their supplies to anyone who hadn't already purchased the exact product twenty times before reaching their stand. The park was a regurgitation of every park in the city, save for the statue that stood in the middle. Liberty stood high above the scene, degraded by the graffiti and urine that clothed her. She kept an eye on the activity.

I stood to the side of the statue, and some 18th Street gang members saw me and said hi. They were raging. Their bodies shook like they had had too much caffeine. Chino, a fierce member of the gang, chatted with Samuel and me. My gaze drifted. To the left, the crazy man who was never clean, pulled his tattered pants a little higher over his bare middle. The rope he had used to tie his pants was frayed. His feet were swollen, and open sores covered them. He had no shoes and hadn't since I had first started crossing the park.

The crazy man looked like Walt Whitman, with

his long matted hair going every which way. He carried a cane, his one possession, wielding it as a weapon. One eye had been gouged out, and the psychotic ravings that dripped from his mouth were made all the more terrifying by his wretched appearance.

The cane went up over Walt's head, and he began his tirade through the park. The cane came close to hitting the many men who sat on the dividing wall drinking their lemonades and beers. They were waiting, biding their time before facing the families that would consume them and their money. They ducked the cane in unison. The one-eyed man was always there, and his ranting was as entertaining as it was dangerous.

As the cane and its carrier exited from view, a new act came to the park. This man had lost his legs. It could have been the war or an accident, I didn't know. His knees were bruised and scratched. His shirt was unbuttoned, exposing his ribs and concave chest, and his unkempt hair was dark and dirty. With his hands propelling him, he inched his way along the wall, paper cup in mouth. The men laughed as one threw him a cólon. It missed the cup, and the legless man scrambled to retrieve it, thanking the laughing bystanders in the course.

Chino's rapid movement drew my attention back to him. He pulled the knife from his shoe and was gone from our conversation fluidly, his movements like a choreographed sequence from a ballet. We turned our heads and followed Chino with our gaze.

A bus had pulled up, and Chino had seen a Salvatrucha member. Chino was on the bus threatening him. Holding a knife to the MS gang member's throat, Chino dared him to debark. The current rules of the street wouldn't permit Chino to kill him on the bus. He had to wait.

Chino came back to us, the knife having disappeared into his shoe, and he picked up the conversation where it had left off. Maybe he'd go to church with us. He'd have to think about it. I sat down while Samuel talked to Snake and her boyfriend. Syringes littered the ground, and a barefoot little girl ran past them.

Two teenage boys walked past the legless man and turned back to gawk. Chuckling, they hit each other on the chest and continued their passage through the park. The crazy man came back into view and hit someone with the cane. The victim was new and unaccustomed to the play. He became enraged and stole the cane away. Walt ran and hid. He was nothing without that cane.

I heard a voice over the crackling speakers that someone had set up. It was yelling. Over the cumbia and salsa music, over the shrieks of the crazy man, over the laughter and screams, it yelled, "You can be saved. Come here and you can be saved." Those who needed that message had not heard it, and Liberty silently continued her watch.

Chapter 26

I can see Payaso's face in my mind's eye. It's a haunting face. His eyes are wild and savage, and they shift in their sockets. He smirks, and his shoulders rise and fall with his morbid laughter. His nose is thin and small. His hair sticks up on his head. His lips form a tight line. He is somehow detached from his body ... a lost soul.

He was a gang member in the Santo Tomas clique of the Salvatrucha. I met him one of the first days I arrived in the Ceiba. He made me uncomfortable immediately because he zoned out and mouthed words only he could hear. He snickered and then laughed, and no one but he knew the joke. He scratched himself behind one ear, and then another, then he reached around and scratched his back. He scratched his legs, arms, and neck as well. He looked like a monkey, twisting to and fro, trying to placate the elusive itch.

He had a tattoo of a demon in the upper right-hand corner of his back. He told me he'd made it himself. He said the demon was his friend. It talked to him, told him what to do, and helped him find the itch. Typically, he pulled his shirt off while talking to me, exposing the demon tattoo. He said the demon told him to do it.

Our conversations never had a set beginning or end. He spoke to me; I responded and asked him questions he rarely answered, and then he would leave, babbling to himself. We never talked more than five minutes at a time.

One day I had to make a phone call, and the phones in the school were out of order. I walked down to the Ceiba, where a public phone was located. After telling the operator who I wanted to call, I waited for him as he dialed the number. He couldn't get through, so I decided to wait until he could try again. When I turned from the counter, Payaso was sitting in a chair in the phone company office.

When I greeted him, he stood up. The wild smirk appeared on his face, his eyes glassed over, and he stared in silence at the wall. This was typical of our meetings, so I was not surprised. A couple other gang members saw me and came in to talk to me as I waited.

We talked about different things, and then one of them told me he would like to go to church. I told him he was welcome to come with me the following morning. He responded, "I can't tomorrow. I've got to do something."

I asked what thing he had to do, and he informed me he had to kill someone.

"I know God will forgive me. That's called grace, right?" I told him God did show grace, but that he didn't mean for people to use it to murder.

He laughed. "Probably not, but I've got to do it. My gang … well, I need revenge. Someone killed my brother. I have to avenge that."

We talked for a long time, debating the finer

points of grace and God, but my Spanish was really inadequate for the situation. I decided to pray. The gang members left, and Payaso and I were left alone. Payaso had been having a private conversation with himself that whole time.

Once he realized we were alone, he leaned over to me and commanded me to give him my shoes. I thought he was joking because he had a smile on his face. The smile, however, was eerie, and his tone became a bit more menacing. "Give them to me now!" I told him I needed my shoes to get back home. I wasn't going to walk barefoot through the town.

Another gang member entered to tell me he was leaving the Ceiba. As I was saying goodbye to him, I felt something. Payaso was bent over, trying to take my shoes off my feet! I kicked my feet out of his hold. He hissed at me to give him the shoes, and I refused. I noticed that Payaso didn't want to draw too much attention to himself because he was whispering about the shoes. I decided to walk outside to where all the gang members were hanging out. I had to drag Payaso with me to make it through the door. Incredibly, he was still trying to get my shoes off my feet!

When we got outside, Gato saw what was happening and started laughing. He approached me, which immediately sent Payaso running. He didn't want to be chastised by his own gang. Payaso headed down the hill and caught a bus to San Salvador.

I never saw him again. I heard he started sniffing glue after his robbery attempts started failing. He lacked the money for the real drugs. His own gang disowned him. They thought he was weird. They would laugh and curse when recalling how Payaso would scratch and talk to himself. It made them as nervous as it had me.

Gato, who had witnessed the attempted shoe caper, looked at my feet and shook his head. "Those are the ugliest shoes I've ever seen. You should throw them away and buy new ones."

He laughed as he told the others what Payaso had done. They all laughed too, agreeing my shoes weren't worth stealing. I looked down at my worn sandals and smiled. I never had made that phone call.

As for the guy who had to kill his brother's murderer, I prayed for him. Others did as well. I ran into him once more, and he told me this story:

"I think you put some curse on me or something. That night, I went to find the guys who had killed my brother. It was pretty dark outside. I used the dark to hide me as I entered enemy territory. I saw some 18th Street member and reached for my gun. I leveled the gun at him, but it wouldn't fire. I checked the bullets, and the gun was loaded. But I couldn't get it to fire. I was so mad.

"I started to back up. I knew it wouldn't be good to be seen by 18th Street without a weapon to protect me. I started to run. I ran and ran. When I stopped, I was out of breath. I didn't know where I was. I looked around to get my bearings. I had stopped in the doorstep of a church. It was the church I had gone to as a little boy. I heard sound coming from inside the doors. They were having an all-night vigil. I went inside. I threw that gun out. I have started going to church again."

Chapter 27

The air was heavy and humid, and I wasn't looking forward to getting all sweaty taking coffee up to the bus drivers. But I had made five pots of it, so I filled my bag with the coffee container, sugar, and sweet bread and walked up the road. When I reached the entrance to the main sector of town, I noticed that people were out of their shacks and watching something with avid interest.

Some of the bus drivers were eating their eggs and beans while standing up, instead of sitting at the usual table. There was a lot of laughing and elbowing. I moved to the first shack for a closer look. Down at the end of the road, two men were brawling. While pouring coffee for the distracted women in the shack, I spilled some of it down my shirt and became even more irritated. I shouldn't have brought coffee. The spill was my confirmation that the day was going to be bad.

I unenthusiastically asked the bus drivers who was fighting and why. They were preoccupied with the fight but managed to let me know that it was two drunks engaged in the ridiculous display. Apparently one of them had accused the other of stealing his alcohol. I shook my head, further lamenting my decision to wake up, and moved on to the next shack. I watched the guys fighting and wasn't quite sure how

I was going to get past them to deliver the coffee to the bus drivers. The drunks were taking up the whole road for this fight.

Having never seen a real fight, it was a disappointment. Fights on movies and television are very pretty, actually. There's perfect choreography, and even missed punches hit the air right. This fight was a let-down from the artistic perspective. More than half their punches landed in dead space, and they kept falling down. It didn't appear they really wanted to fight because they stopped periodically to breathe and probably to gather their strength and settle their stomachs.

I sighed loudly. I was very perturbed that I was going to have to walk through them or around them or figure out some new path. I wasn't in the mood to think. I wanted to give the microbuseros the coffee and go back to bed.

I gathered my bag up and began to walk toward the fighters. I glanced at the spectators and rolled my eyes. They chuckled, and some asked what I was going to do. I grumbled that I didn't know and kept walking.

When I reached the drunken men, I saw how bloody and ragged they looked. They stunk, not only of sweat and alcohol, but also of dirt and blood. The older drunk saw me and stopped fighting. He took off his hat and patted down his hair. The younger one followed suit. They separated from each other and very calmly greeted me, "Good morning, Mother." I told them good morning and invited them for coffee as soon as they finished pummeling each other. They graciously accepted and waited until I passed and was a safe distance from them before resuming their fight.

There was an explosion of laughter from the bus drivers. They couldn't believe the men had stopped the fight to let me pass. I poured the coffee and handed out the bread, and we watched the fight from the depot. It eventually ended with no victor. It was one of those days when we should have all stayed in bed.

Unfortunately, the day didn't get much better, and sleeping wasn't an option for me. I had a meeting to attend in town, so I readied myself and departed for Parque Libertad. Upon arriving, I noticed that the girls from 18th Street were perched on the raised platform in the park discussing plans and talking about the mundane things of life. Hammer complimented Bugs's hair, and Ghost showed off her new tattoo. They laughed and talked about their kids. Several male gangsters walked by and joked with the girls, and some even had the girls run errands for them. It was a laid-back day.

I crossed the street after debarking from the bus and stood below them in silence. I was waiting for someone, and the girls didn't like me that much anyway. I was tired, too, having spent the afternoon in sweltering buses visiting different gang members after having hauled the coffee to the bus drivers and teaching my English classes that morning. Gato was grumpy and hadn't talked to me, so I was aggravated and not in the mood for pleasantries or the lack thereof.

Lobo hurried over to me when he saw me. He greeted me and brought me some water to drink. Maniaco had ordered Lobo to protect me whenever I was in the park. I appreciated the gesture, even though Lobo hated being a babysitter. I liked Lobo because he always made me laugh. He and I were discussing the weather and his new tattoo when a guy from 18th Street swaggered by us. The girl with him was scantily dressed and giggled loudly. It probably would have been no big deal if Ghost hadn't seen them.

When Ghost started to cuss, I jerked my attention toward the platform where the girls were standing. I asked Lobo what was happening, but he ignored me and stayed focused on the disturbance. The guy and his girl yelled some things back to Ghost and then flipped her off as they crossed the street.

Ghost began to cry, and the girls hugged her and told her things would be okay. Lobo filled me in excitedly as he continued to watch the scene playing out before us. The guy was Ghost's boyfriend, the father of her unborn baby. To walk into the park with a new girl and parade her in front of Ghost was a blatant disrespect. I was sucked into the drama and curiously watched Ghost to see what would happen.

Hammer, Bugs, Snake, and Tiny were all offering Ghost their support and a few solid insults to hurl at her lover. Ghost rose to her feet and wiped her eyes. She half-cried, half-screamed that he wouldn't get away with disrespecting her, and she reached for her knife.

My eyes widened, and I glanced at Lobo. As the

girls ran across the street to catch up with Ghost's lover, Lobo thought about it for a split second, decided the fight would be better than protecting me from it, grabbed my arm, and pulled me over to the action as well.

When we got there, Ghost had the knife pointed at her boyfriend's throat. His new girlfriend cowered behind him and whimpered. All the gang girls stood behind Ghost as a display of force. I wondered if they supported her to give themselves a sense of pride and dignity. They slept with whomever wanted them because it was part of the rules. They had all been cheated on, left behind, and passed to the next guy. When they stood behind Ghost and her knife, their ferocity was tangible.

Lobo stood in front of me, shielding me from danger. He was laughing as he heard the exchange between Ghost and the guy. I told Lobo it wasn't right to disrespect the girls so much. He acknowledged that but said it was hard not to when a new beautiful girl walked past them.

Ghost was crying and shaking. She took the knife away from his neck several times and took comfort from her friends. The guy stayed there, waiting for the knife to return to his neck, and it always did. By now a huge group of gang members had gathered, and they chose sides. Was Ghost being too harsh, or should the guy pay the penalty for disrespect? Almost down the line, male gang members sided with Ghost's lover. They saw themselves in him. Female gang members sided with Ghost for the same reason.

The knife was once again at his throat, when Ghost finally dissolved into tears and commanded him to leave the park. He left with his girlfriend as if he'd been waiting all along for Ghost's permission. The crowd disbanded shortly thereafter, and Ghost was left holding the knife, and with it, a small piece of her soul.

Chapter 28

In the Ceiba, we waited for Psycho to show up. He was new to the park, had touted himself as an OG, and wanted to take control of the clique. The other gang members respected him immediately. Anyone who had spent time in Los Angeles was treated with reverence in the gang realm. After all, LA was the gang capital of the world.

Gato had told me there was a new leader of the MS. He had said I should meet him because he spoke English. Saddened to learn that an OG had moved to Santo Tomas, I had gone to find out about him.

Psycho comprehended nothing as I addressed him in English. He stopped the one-sided conversation I was having with him, citing the need to speak Spanish, so his homeboys could know what was being said. I knew it was because he didn't speak a word of English. He punctuated our Spanish conversation with an English curse word or "understand?" but there was nothing else to substantiate his story about having lived in the United States for five years.

He was vague when I asked him where he lived in Los Angeles. He feigned confusion when I made some cultural point about the U.S. And whenever I said anything in English, Psycho asserted quite loudly that I should speak in Spanish for everyone to hear. Basically, Psycho knew that I knew he wasn't for real, and he was trying desperately to save face in front of the Santo Tomas clique.

I told Gato what I thought, and he laughed. He didn't know what to believe. He was excited by the idea of having a "real" gang member take on the clique, guiding it to new levels of acceptance and danger. On the other hand, Psycho had usurped Gato's and Oso's authority by coming in with the Los Angeles story.

Gato called Psycho over to us and asked Psycho to speak to me in English. Psycho attempted to look good. He said some English words, but they meant nothing lumped together as they were. It was a disjointed list of vocabulary words that one might have learned from an English 1 primer: book, cat, house, grass. Psycho looked at me triumphantly and turned to walk away.

Gato asked me what was said, and I confessed that the conversation had made no sense and that I still believed Psycho was a liar. Gato agreed but said no one else cared. Everyone in the Santo Tomas clique wanted to be accepted by the San Salvador cliques. In order to be accepted, they had to show more commitment to the gang. They needed to rob, kill, maim, whatever, to be considered legitimate. The boys believed Psycho would help them do it.

Psycho and his pompous proclamations irritated me. The boys from Santo Tomas, my friends, were making me angry. I felt disgust for their evil ambitions. I was furious at the whole situation.

A few weeks later, on my coffee run to the bus depot, Psycho appeared dressed in the cobrador's uniform. He told me he had gotten a job on the 21 bus route. Speaking English, I offered him coffee. He looked confused. I showed him the cup, and he said he would like some. I must admit I wanted Psycho to look bad. I wanted everyone to see him as a fraud. I was worried about the boys in my town and what Psycho was going to lead them into. Psycho knew I distrusted him. I was sure Gato had told him, if my attitude hadn't already given me away. We were not friends.

The weeks that followed were horrible. The MS boys got drunk every day and bought drugs from one of Psycho's friends. Psycho had gotten Papaya, a fellow gang member, pregnant. There were altercations over stupid things all over the town. Oso shot someone who had offended him. Gato went on binges, refusing to come to work for days at a time. Several gang members stabbed a young 18th Street member on the street where I lived. It was ugly, and it only served to make me hate Psycho more.

I had to change my way of doing things with the MS boys. Working with them one on one, I talked to them and shared things with them individually instead of in a group setting. I visited them in jail, talked to their parents, and carried them home when they were too drunk to be alone.

Psycho thought all was going well in Santo Tomas. He was pleased with the boys' progress. Finally, I went to talk directly to him. He suggested we play basketball, and I agreed. I had played with all the other guys many times before, so this was not a new phenomenon. We walked to the basketball courts, only silence between us.

Psycho made a bet with me. He suggested that if he won, I would pay him $25, but if I won, he would go to church with me for a month of Sundays. I am sorry to say I lost after a tight match. He out-shot me. I paid my wager, and we sat down to talk.

I asked him what he thought about all the boys being drunk and high. He told me it wasn't a help to his plans. He said he couldn't get them to do anything when they were passed out. I understood his logic, and I asked him what his plans were. He told me he wanted to recruit new members and bulk up the army of gang members. He wanted to expand the clique's territory into Santiago Texacuango, 18th Street territory.

We discussed the stabbing that had taken place earlier that month. Laughing, he told me it was a sad thing. He flippantly explained to me it had to be done, and the same thing would have happened if the situation had been reversed.

I apologized for not liking him, not so much because I liked him then any better than before, but because I shouldn't have felt the way I did. He needed the same help as every other gang member. He acted surprised but accepted my apology. I told him I disagreed with his plans and disapproved of the negative influence he was bringing into Santo Tomas. He said he wasn't going to be a gang member for too much longer, since Papaya was going to have their baby. I didn't believe him. He liked the power he had with this group of guys, but I said nothing.

After that conversation, Psycho and I remained civil. Things got a little better in Santo Tomas. My boys began to mainstream quicker than I had thought possible. They became more belligerent and territorial, but the substance abuse was slowing down.

Papaya did have her baby. She stopped coming to gang meetings. She was a wife and mother now, and it was not acceptable to do both. Psycho continued working for the bus line during the day and running the gang by night. However, his plans never did work out. Eighteenth Street held their ground, and Santiago Texacuango remained their territory. Many members of the MS in Santo Tomas retired and left the gang. The clique fragmented and went its separate ways. The more serious gangsters jumped into cliques in San Salvador. Others stayed in the Ceiba flashing signs and not doing a whole lot else. Thankfully, Psycho's ambitions had been as false as his stories about Los Angeles. For that, I am eternally grateful.

Chapter 29

I really never got too involved in gang business. I wasn't a gang member, nor did I want to be. I was a missionary and did not feel it was my place to know too much about what was going on. But on two occasions, I did enter the dirty world of gang life, and both times, it was in Gato's defense. The first time, I almost got killed, while pleading for mercy for Gato from an 18th Street gang member whom I had overheard plotting his murder. The second time, I was up against his own homeboys.

Restless and anxious, Diablo was always looking for action. He wanted something to happen in Santo Tomas, with his clique, in his life, anything at all. Being a young male in a rough neighborhood would make this a dangerous enough proposition, but Diablo had the added bonus of being a gang member. He liked to party, wanted to fight, and was bored enough to be a menace.

I knew him from the bus line. He was a cobrador and a friend of mine. He drank his coffee and then grabbed my arm and pulled me off to talk to him, always with such urgency that it became a joke. He'd lean over to me and begin long conversations of nothings that he tried to make seem important. He tried enchanting me with gang secrets and regaled me with stories of his burgeoning gang reputation.

I liked Diablo because he was polite, generous, and fun to be around. I saw a lot of potential in him. I knew of his wild side, but I had never seen it personally. I discovered it in a most tragic way.

"Have you seen Diablo?" Gato was frantic when he asked me. I told him I hadn't seen him since the day before. I asked why, and Gato revealed that someone had been stabbed in Santiago Texacuango. The victim was an 18th Street gang member. I asked Gato if Diablo had done it. He didn't confirm or deny it. By that, I knew Diablo had been involved.

I asked Gato why he was so anxious to find Diablo. Typically, gang members didn't show much concern for their homeboys when they got in trouble. I found that interesting, since gang members claimed to be family. Gato said the police had come looking for him. He didn't want to go to jail for something he hadn't done. He thought Diablo should say something. Gato was irritated that he was being blamed for Diablo's crime.

I tried to find Diablo myself. Gato was my favorite person in El Salvador, so the thought of him being in jail was intolerable. I frantically began my investigation by scouring jails, seeking out gang members, and as subtly as possible, eliciting information about what had happened. I located Oso and asked him to keep his eyes open for me. He told me he would. I also asked the bus drivers to alert me if Diablo showed up.

When I arrived at the Ceiba, I found Muñeca, a new MS recruit. After a little conversation, she let me know what had happened with the stabbing. She had been there and had participated. Diablo had the knife and had led the group. She shared the details readily.

A group of MS members went to Santiago Texacuango to hang out. When they were returning on the bus, they noticed that the guy sitting on the back of the bus was 18th Street. Muñeca said she had wanted to go home and just ignore him, but Diablo wanted to mess with the guy. His reasoning was that if the situation had been reversed, 18th Street wouldn't hesitate to fight.

They waited for the kid to get off the bus, and then they debarked. Diablo yelled out, "Mara Salvatrucha," and they descended upon the lone boy like a pack of wolves on their prey. Muñeca said the kid didn't even yell back 18th Street. He had wanted peace. He wanted to get away.

They beat him up and stabbed him several times. Diablo had made each of the others stab the boy. It was a proof of loyalty. Muñeca grew strangely quiet after telling me the story. "I feel sad and sort of different. But I guess we had to do it."

I asked her why she thought they had no choice. She said there would be no respect for the MS clique if they hadn't done something to the boy. She didn't want her gang to be shamed. She didn't want to be responsible for that. I asked her how she felt about Diablo. "He did what he had to do. He was happy afterwards. I wasn't, but I'm a girl…we feel differently than men."

I left Muñeca, disturbed, yet happy to know the

truth, and anxious to find Diablo. I tracked him down later that night. This time *I* grabbed *his* arm and pulled him over to talk.

I informed him I knew what had happened. He feigned ignorance, but I persisted, and he finally admitted it. I asked him what he was going to do. He said there was nothing to do. I explained to him that Gato was being questioned by the police for this stabbing, that the boy might die, and that Gato could go to jail for life. I was fuming while I pleaded for Diablo to do the right thing. He could see I was mad as I challenged his loyalty to his friend and gang.

Diablo responded angrily and defensively. He ridiculed me as he asked me what I wanted from him. When I yelled at him that I wanted him to get Gato off the hook, he expressed amusement at my obvious ignorance, stating that the police wouldn't do anything to Gato. I wasn't so sure. Through force of habit, he shook my hand even though he was livid for my intrusion into his life and told me he had to go. I reminded him to do the right thing as he cockily strolled away from me.

Luckily, the boy who had been stabbed started to recover a few weeks later. He identified Diablo as the leader of the group and cleared Gato for the violent act. The police dropped their charges against Gato and began their search for Diablo.

When he heard that the police were looking for him, Diablo moved to another city and started to drink and do drugs non-stop. He began hanging out with members of organized crime groups and got involved in all those things he believed would bring him excitement and purpose. On one such day, drunken and bored, Diablo ripped a gun out of one of his friend's hands. In the struggle that ensued, a shot was fired, and Diablo lost his eye.

The day Diablo returned to work on the bus line, he looked sad and humiliated. His smile, once so ready, now hid. His one good eye stayed downcast. He shuffled along. It was distressing to see him that way.

I gave Diablo a hug. He made a joke about his glass eye that wasn't funny and probably wasn't meant to be. He swore to me that if Gato had been arrested, he had planned on coming forward. I think he needed to show himself, more than me, that there was still honor in him, that there was still purpose in his life.

Diablo's smile returned tentatively. He joked, partied, and touted his eye patch as a badge of honor. The police had apparently given up their search for Diablo because I never heard a thing about the stabbing again. Diablo seemed normal again. Normal, except for the way he held his head. Now, instead of the proud stance he once had, he held his head to one side, a self-conscious tilt. It was the price he paid for his boredom.

Chapter 30

"Kylla, thanks for helping out with Diablo. You didn't have to do it."

"Yeah, but I love you, kiddo. And you should know it by now."

Every time I told him I loved him, Gato looked at me strangely and then smiled and looked away. We hung out in the Ceiba and swapped stories for the afternoon. Neither one of us had to work, nor did we have any place to go. It was a relaxing, lackadaisical day, and as we leaned back against the bench by the giant tree, we let our words spill out.

"Gato, I'm gonna tell you something, and you have to tell me if you know this person. I think you might, and I want you to finish her story."

So I told my story on that warm afternoon as the occasional wind blew my hair and cooled me off for a moment at a time.

Her eyes were so heavily outlined with black eyeliner that it was hard to identify where the makeup started and eye ended. Her skin was pale and her features delicate. Her brown hair was short and curly. Her thin body, though covered beneath oversized clothes, added to her exotic appearance. She was truly striking.

Two guys were with her, adorning either side. They were wearing baggy clothes too, and their eyes revealed the bloodthirstiness that was in their hearts. They looked tough, but they were no comparison to the girl between them. She was like an exquisite marble statue, beautiful but cold.

She was notably the leader. As they walked down that street, with its potholes and piles of rubble, the boys looking over their shoulders, and her looking straight ahead, it was clear they had a mission to complete. At her command, the boys split up, positioning themselves on the two streets. They crouched down in anticipation of the fight that would most surely ensue.

She walked right past me. She looked into the bus where I was sitting and arched her eyebrow. I smiled, unsure of what she might do, struck by her beauty. She flipped me off and kept walking. I looked out at the two boys. They stayed in position, anger and hatred distorting their faces.

I turned around in the bus to watch. She walked into a group of teenage boys, students from a local high school. She shoved one of them before flashing the MS sign and screaming, "Mara Salvatrucha, assholes!" Her statement electrified the group. They dropped their backpacks and started screaming, "Eighteen!" and flashing their signs, more as an encouragement to each other than as an offense to her.

She raced back up the street, and her comrades began throwing chunks of cement and building rubble at the oncoming students. She turned to face the angry mob and flashed Salvatrucha again and again, laughing as the rocks flew past her. She bent down, retrieving some of the stones herself, and hurled them.

When she motioned to her fellow soldiers, they ran to her sides and retreated, all the while, throwing the remaining blocks of rock and cement. The students stopped their pursuit when the three attackers turned the corner and disappeared.

I looked around as the dust cleared. The bus I sat in had sustained a few nicks during the fight. Thankfully, none of the rocks had broken the glass. A mother and her young daughter had been caught in the middle of the war. They huddled together in a doorframe. When it ended, they dusted themselves off and continued their journey to the store.

I heard sirens. Police cars came screeching to a halt beside the students. They recounted the story of the mysterious girl and her friends. The police knew who it was by the description. Her tag was Muerta, and she had proven herself a fierce defender of the Salvatrucha gang. She had killed many times, and subsequently moved up the ranks in the gang, despite the fact that she was a girl. Her expressionless eyes were her trademarks, a giveaway when it came to identifying her. The police dismissed the students and began their fruitless search for Muerta and her henchmen.

My bus pulled out, and as we traveled the back roads of San Salvador, I saw her again. She boarded a bus and blended in with the horde of passengers. The cops drove past the corner on which she had been standing only moments before. They shook their heads in frustration, turned off their sirens, and drove away.

"That wasn't the last time I saw her. I saw her in the Ceiba one day. She really made an impression on me."

Gato's eyes had been closed as he listened to my story. He nodded his head when I finished.

"I knew her. I'll finish your story now."

Muerta boarded a bus to go home one night after robbing someone on the street. She noticed that the two guys sitting behind her were 18th Street gang members. She stayed calm, but asked the cobrador to let her off at the next stop. When the bus stopped and Muerta stepped out onto the street, they shot her several times in the back. She died facedown on the pavement, cold and unfeeling, not much different from her life. With her last breath, her haunting beauty faded from reality to legend.

"That's awful, Gato."

"Yeah."

We sat in silence for a few minutes before Gato got up and bought us some Cokes.

"Here, now keep going with the stories."

"Okay, Gatito…I'm going to tell you about a really great person who changed his life."

"Oh, God, another sermon."

"Shut up."

Pantera had been an MS member and soldier for an organized crime group in Los Angeles and later in San Salvador. He'd been in the gang for a long time. Pantera was respected, honored, and admired by his homeboys. He was the proverbial big man on campus.

He became a Christian and left the gang behind, no small feat for someone whose life *was* the gang. He got a job selling electronics. He went to church. He witnessed to his old homeboys. His testimony was evident. Pantera replaced his gun with a Bible.

Pantera traveled to jails and parks on weekends, where he shared Christ with inmates and gang members. He preached in revivals and crusades. He served his fellow man. He even worked up the courage to talk with active 18th Street gang members—something that could have gotten him killed. He did it all for God.

His beaten body was found on the side of the road. He'd been shot three times. The three bullets formed a triangle on his body, a triangle identical to the tattoo so many gang members shared, a triangle that symbolized "mi vida loca."[42]

His wounds sent a message. "There's no way out. A gang member is always a gang member. You *will* pay with your life if you turn your back on the clique. God cannot save you. You'll die for your crazy life."

Pantera lay still on the side of the road, his white shirt soaked with blood. His pants and tie were dirty and crumpled. He was dead. His Bible had been thrown out of the car along with his body, a final disgrace.

They thought they had won. They had killed the traitorous Pantera for turning to God. They laughed and moved on to other business. But they hadn't won. Pantera lives. He lives with the Father who saved him from his crazy life. He lives and rejoices and sits at his Father's feet. His crazy life ended many years before; his physical life ceased not too long ago, but his real life has just begun.

"And you think *that's* a good story? All you're telling me is that there was no point of him leaving the gang. They killed him anyway."

"I didn't say that. I just wanted you to see that there were other examples of people who have left the gang."

"Yeah, but he's dead."

"Yeah, but he was willing to die for the truth, and you're just willing to die for nothing. There's a difference."

"Tell me something else, Vaga. I'm bored with that story."

I closed my eyes and sat back and remembered another time when a fellow missionary and I bought all the chocolates a little boy was selling on the street one stifling afternoon in downtown San Salvador. He looked at us, first suspicious of our request, then exhilarated by the prospect. He took our money, and we took the chocolates, handing him one as we walked away. I marveled at the discipline of such a little kid being able to resist the chocolates day in and day out, selling them but never eating them. He sucked on the chocolate we gave him, licking the paper for any remnants left there. He was blissful.

We boarded a bus and sat in the back. As people filled in the seats, we passed them chocolates. Each person smiled and thanked us, and some even started to talk to us. When the bus stopped in traffic, we threw chocolate down to the people on the street. They looked up laughing and shaking their heads at the crazy gringos who were flinging chocolate about.

We felt like royalty throwing those chocolates to the four corners of the wind. Old men smiled toothless grins. Women placed the chocolate in their pockets for later. Children tore into their candies and wolfed them down, sometimes asking for more. Teenagers, gang members, vendors, and shoppers all reacted the same. Our humanness was evident; chocolate was our common ground.

"Now that's a cool story, Loca. I also remember the time you brought those two street kids to the downtown bus depot. Do you remember that?"

"Yeah, you tell me that story."

I sat back and remembered the story along with Gato that evening. His half-smile spread into a full one as we reminisced.

They were dirty and disheveled. Barefoot and pitiful, they stood on the corner asking for money. Within a few minutes they had received several cólones. It was obvious they were gluesniffers. The crusted, yellow crumbs that dotted their clothes and hair proved that. They continued begging for money, becoming elated with every clank as the coins dropped into the can.

People typically ignored the gluesniffers, not wanting to support their deadly habit. But these two boys were different, and the mothers that walked past them couldn't stand their plight. They were only about seven years old.

They were two young boys who made the street their home, who didn't know a mother's love or a father's discipline. Two first-graders who would never go to school, never know the joy of reading. Two kids whose teachers were the gang members and street people, whose family was the band of gluesniffers they'd met. Two boys who would probably die before they turned eighteen, having never really lived.

As I watched them, two young men crossed the street and demanded the money from those little boys. The men slapped them when they asked to keep a cólon for themselves. The men left, laughing, counting their loot, moving on to their next victims.

I got angry and walked over to the boys. I asked them what happened, and they explained to me that they were paying their dues. The boys believed the men owned the street, and they had to pay rent to beg. They asked me for money. I told them to follow me.

I bought them pupusas and Cokes at the bus depot. Gato and some of the other bus drivers talked to the boys like big brothers, giving them advice, chastising them for being dirty, making them laugh. Gato asked me how I thought they managed out on the street, alone and penniless. I said I didn't know. He raised his eyebrow at me and gave me an odd look. I didn't know what his look was supposed to imply. At that moment I didn't have time to analyze it.

Gato told the boys some jokes, and they laughed heartily. After they polished off the pupusas, Gato went to the little food stand and bought them both more pupusas and some chips and sweet bread they could take with them. They stuffed their pockets full. Gato told them to save it for when they were really hungry and didn't know when they would eat again. He also told them they could come by the bus stop to drink water when they were thirsty. They both sat next to him on the little cement curb from where he was lecturing them.

He whispered something in one of their ears. The boy chuckled and shook his head. He told his companion, who laughed too. Looking at him with a challenging glance, Gato yelled, "Do it!"

The little boy stuffed the last bit of pupusa in his mouth and ran over to me and latched onto my leg. I was knocked slightly off balance by the sudden impact. The bus drivers erupted with laughter. Looking down at the boy, I asked him what he was doing. He just gazed up at me with soulful innocent eyes, while clutching my leg with all his might, and stuttered that Gato had put him up to it.

I turned around with the boy attached to me and playfully shot Gato a dirty look. He slapped his knee and laughed. He told the other boy to get me on the other side, but thankfully he was shy, and instead of gluing himself to me, he requested a kiss. I kissed his cheek. When the leg-holder saw that his friend had a better idea than had Gato, he released me and received his kiss on the cheek as well.

An hour passed, and I needed to get home. Gato guaranteed that he would take care of the boys, and that I should go.

"It's fine, Kylla. I understand the type of lives they have. I'll take care of them for you."

Gato explained to the boys I had to go. They expressed that they had to go back to their post anyway, or else the street owners would get mad. After giving me hugs, hand in hand, they walked out onto the street, barefoot and alone.

Gato sighed as he finished the story. He glanced over at me, and I returned his gaze.

"Gato, you are a good guy, and for that I love you. Who would believe that a gang member would be so sweet to a couple of kids?"

Gato's smile returned, and he manuevered our conversation onto another subject.

"Kylla, tell me about how you met the MS kids from Mejicanos. They're from my gang, so I should know."

I nodded to him and thought back to a day months ago when I had gone in search of two gang members who were more hungry than threatening. I'd met the boys in Wendy's, where they were attempting to sell gum to the customers. As they devoured the hamburgers I purchased, they choked out between mouthfuls that they lived in Mejicanos, one of the poorest sectors of San Salvador. I felt like God had put them directly in my path for a reason, so I knew I had to go find and visit them again.

I boarded three different buses in my quest to find them and finally leapt off the bus at the Pollo Campero[43] in Mejicanos because the bus had not completely stopped and was continuing down its path at a slow roll. Because the directions they'd given me were vague, I had to ask people on the street if they knew Sadface and Homer. The sneering group of people I asked pointed to their left. They instructed me to follow the path down to the hell where the boys lived.

I followed the sloping, insufficient road, at times turning my feet to the side to avoid falling on the rubble that gave way with every step. I made it down to where the road leveled out. A young, unkempt boy sat on a chipped curb and ordered me to tell him who I was. After introducing myself, I made it clear I was looking for Sadface and Homer. He eyed me suspiciously and told me to wait.

The child ran around the corner and was gone. As directed, I sat down on the curb and waited. To my right stood a wall from a demolished building— a monument to the Salvatrucha. I saw Sadface and Homer's tag names spray-painted on the wall, along with twenty others, including "Cero Mota," "Chucky," and "Lil Rascal." A few minutes later, Homer appeared with the child in tow. He greeted me and excitedly asked me to follow him to his home.

He adeptly maneuvered down dangerously steep stairs, over a tree stump, through a man-made stream, into a mildewed, graffittied, overrun patch of earth they called home. I stumbled down the same path, not as accustomed. The homeboys used an English word to describe their house, a destroyer.

The four cement walls were chipped and corroded. The tin roof and door had holes in them, making it incredibly uncomfortable during the rainy season.

The floor was dirt, and four flea-bitten, soiled, gutted mattresses served as their beds. They had one pot and one cup. The bathroom was outside. They were supposed to relieve themselves to the right of the shack, but when in a drunken or drug-induced stupor, they couldn't tell left from right.

The stench of urine and feces was unbearable during the heat of the day, so they stayed away as much as possible. Glue bags adorned the beaten-down foliage. Chip bags and cigarette butts speckled the dirt, giving it an almost festive look with the array of color they provided. The boys told me to be careful where I stepped. Cero Mota had not done clean-up that day, and they would have to punish him.

Nine of them lived in this pit, ranging in age from ten to seventeen. All the gang members I'd ever encountered had claimed to be in the gang for a number of reasons. Without exception, they had joined because the gang felt like family to them. However, it was only in the case of these boys that it rang especially true, because besides one another, they had no one.

They had lost their parents, been left, or had left home. They lacked education, friends, jobs; they only had each other. They disciplined one another, fought each other, defended each other, supported and loved one another. They may have had different last names and backgrounds, but the 13 they proudly displayed made them family.

Sadface arrived at the house a little later. He was drunk, having spent his wages on the cheapest alcohol available. He gave his last cólon to the other boys, who, in turn, fought over how to spend it. They needed toilet paper, but churros sounded good, too.

I gave them the food I had brought, and we ate, talked, and got to know one another. Sadface tried to hit on me and got angry when I told him to leave me alone. He stood and threw up, then left the group. Ignoring him, the other guys kept eating. They asked me to pray for them. They were scared. My heart wept for these motherless boys. They saw no way out, and they were old beyond their years.

We prayed, and as they escorted me back to the bus stop, they begged me to come back. They told me I didn't have to bring them food, just come back. The tattoos and baggy clothes were out of place on their bodies. These were not gang members; they were little homeless boys. They beamed at me, and I smiled back. They reminded me to return. And I did.

I fell silent after finishing the story. I stared up into the branches of the giant Ceiba tree as they shielded us from the sun. Gato glanced at me, then joined me in my examination of the tree.

"But you already know that, Gato. I go every week, and sometimes it's so bad there ... "

Gato looked at me questioningly, so I told him another story.

The boys in Mejicanos were drunk. They were crying when Samuel and I got there. I carried the weekly supplies I had purchased into the shack and set them down. Between the tears, they thanked me for the supply of beans, rice, soap, toothpaste, and cookies.

I asked them what was wrong. They looked ragged and tired. It didn't seem right that these young boys should have the look of old men who have seen too much in their lifetimes. But that was the reality.

Their ribs were sticking out. Several of them were dirty. The water had been out in their neighbor's house, where they were usually permitted to bathe, so they hadn't been able to wash themselves in the cement washbasin. They itched.

Chelito told me that one of their friends had died. He had hanged himself. He hadn't thought this was much of a life and thought death might be more merciful.

Chucky and Lil Rascal were crying as well, and I hugged them. They hadn't known the boy who killed himself, so I thought it was odd they were crying so hard. I asked them to tell me what they were feeling.

"There's no hope in this life. Each week, someone else dies, and you know it's true. What do we have? Nothing ... we *are* nothing."

I was silenced by their statements. The depression and death in their shack was palpable. There was always a tragedy. Their lives were stunted, suffocated, and worst of all, ignored.

These boys weren't pretty. They were sad specimens. Morally, they were dying, not from deadened hearts, but from desperation. If they needed food, they stole it. If they needed to forget, they drank or sniffed the glue. If they needed to feel good, they found a girl. It was simple, and it made sense to them.

They lived in appalling conditions. They were at

the mercy of their neighbors for a plate to eat off of, a cup to drink from, and a cement washbasin in which to clean themselves.

They lacked education. They lacked everything really. But what seemed to affect them most was the lack of concern from the rest of the world. No one cared. No one even looked at them twice, except to clutch their purses closer or shoo them away.

What could I tell them? How could I assure them they were special and loved? My words were hollow. They made me ill because I heard the echo of them as they bounced against hearts and minds they could not penetrate.

Chelito begged for Samuel and me to pray for them. As we began to pray, the boys wiped their tears. Their heads bowed, they prayed harder than I'd seen others do. The sheer determination they demonstrated to have God's protection must have impressed God.

When we finished praying, I gathered up the boys, and we went to eat pupusas. We sat and talked. They told us about the week. Homer and Sadface had joined us, and they ate aggressively. Lil Rascal asked for a second Coke, and Chelito yelled at him for being rude. I got the second Coke, and Chelito took it from Lil Rascal and drank some.

Chucky said he had to go. He had to meet with someone down the road. He thanked us for the food and left. Cero Mota came by, and they gave him the last pupusa. He was only ten. Chelito messed his hair up like any big brother should.

I looked at these boys with an incredible respect.

They survived things weekly that we often don't experience in a lifetime. They had nothing. No one cared about them. And for all of their problems, addictions, anger, and sadness, I think the world is lacking some beauty and depth by not knowing and embracing them.

Gato cleared his throat as my voice got quieter at the end of the story.

"That was my life, Kylla. And sometimes I feel just like they do. I don't think I want to hear any more today. There is too much sadness in the world."

"You're right, Gato. But there is hope."

"That's what you tell me...but enough stories...let's eat."

I wanted to keep talking, but it was obvious to me that he did not. This always happened with us. When we started to get into a serious conversation that would have allowed me to know him more deeply, he would cut me off, and I was frustrated. I just looked at Gato, his face calm and restful by my side. He looked innocently into my disappointed face, and I knew we were done for the day.

Chapter 31

The day I read in an American magazine that El Salvador had been ranked number one in the world for per capita homicides, I had to go out and see some gang members. I took the bus downtown and commented to some of the microbuseros about the murderous statistic. They laughed and said they believed it. They called it population control.

I asked Douglas to let me off at Parque Libertad, and he pulled his bus over to the curb, told me to be careful, and said goodbye. There was always something happening in the park, and it kept life interesting. As I walked, a skinny woman with wispy blonde hair and two different color eyes twirled in circles in the street and chanted, "The demons are here. The demons are with you. The demons are here." I snapped at her to be quiet in Jesus' name, and she fell silent, although she continued to spin.

As I crossed the park, a guttural cry caused me to jerk to attention. The hair on my neck stood up, and I didn't know what to do. He was coming at me with rage as his guide, and the hatred he felt stabbed me. His words were explosive and directed at me, "Gringa bitch, get out…"

There were no gang members around to help me, and everyone else just watched. It seemed to be happening in slow motion, and I didn't know what to do.

I kept walking, trying to avoid eye contact, not knowing how it would end.

He charged toward me, and I thought back to when I had been confronted by other people who hated me because of my nationality. I had apologized for whatever my countrymen had done. Knowing there was a lot of racism and hurt in the world, I never blamed people for being upset. I figured there was a reason.

However, it didn't look like the man coming at me wanted to talk. As he neared me, he raised his fist. At that moment, his two friends came and grabbed him away. He shrieked and wept and fought his friends, trying to get at me. His friends told him I was different; that I swept the park and treated the people well. They told him to save his anger for someone else. I passed the three men and waited in a store until he and his friends went to a bar to relax and have a drink. But he had succeeded. His whimpers, not his fists, had landed me a devastating blow.

When I was sure I would be safe and my heart had stopped beating so quickly, I walked to the Christian bookstore where I had originally been headed before my meeting with the Mejicanos Salvatrucha members. Something caught my eye; perhaps it was the rapid movement or the way everyone dropped their heads down and hurried past. I looked to my right, and a human sandwich made me stop and stare.

A boy was caught between three others. One was in front of him and two were behind him, hindering an escape. It was like watching some horrible television program that shouldn't be on prime time but always has a wide audience.

The one in front stabbed the boy in the middle. She was smiling as she jabbed the knife into his stomach and jerked it upwards. People kept walking. The men who sat directly in front of the scene drinking their lemonades craned their necks to see the boy drop as the three ran away. The stabbed boy got up, too. He ran as best he could with his blood dotting a trail behind him. I kept walking, my head shaking and my mouth dry.

Later, in the evening, as I returned to the park after meeting with the MS boys in Mejicanos, I encountered a few 18th Street gangsters. They were new to me, but one of them knew about me. He bought me a juice from one of the vendors I swept for and asked me if I had heard about Bugs. I shook my head no. He liked knowing something I didn't and leaned back and stretched. We sat in silence for a couple of minutes, my cue to beg for information.

"Please tell me what happened. I haven't seen her for weeks, and I just want to know how she is. Can you please tell me?"

Once my begging was finished, and his authority sufficiently acknowledged, he leaned in and whispered in my ear.

The buzz on the street was that Bugs was in green light. Maniaco thought she was fraternizing with Salvatrucha members. It was highly unlikely in my mind, but what did I know? The word was out; Bugs was fair game.

Apparently, Maniaco had assigned someone the task of taking her out, a perverted show of loyalty to the master. It was rumored that Ghost, her best friend, had been given the job. She could choose some helpers, but she was the boss with this errand.

Street lore holds that Bugs was only identifiable by her tattoos. Her body had been mutilated, eyes cut out, breasts slashed. She died alone in a pool of her own blood, in the "wrong" neighborhood. No one spoke of it or was allowed to shed a tear. They heard the message loud and clear: total allegiance to the number that adorned their bodies.

Chapter 32

Gato stopped working for some time. He was on a drinking binge, a precursor to what lay ahead. To be honest, I was disappointed in him. He possessed an incredible charisma that others sought out, and in my opinion, he was throwing it away. I blamed Psycho and his stupid influence, but I was really angry with Gato.

I am embarrassed to say that I turned my attention to helping other people and excluded him. I began to think in terms of how many people I could actually impact for the better, rather than in further developing relationships that didn't have any potential for return. After all, I reasoned deceptively to myself, wasn't that more mature of me as a missionary? I mean, most of the churches and Christians I had encountered always wanted to know how many people I had "brought into the kingdom." They were never interested in how many friends I had.

So in my pride and stupidity, I went that route for a time, and Gato didn't make the cut. I had seen no changes in him. He was still as wild and bad as ever. He had no intention of leaving the gang. He was now drinking excessively and talking about getting into organized crime. I needed to focus my time and energy elsewhere.

Oso was the lucky recipient of my misguided

godly fervor. I sought him out and spent the bulk of my time with him. I became very concerned with his well-being and his salvation. I didn't realize that the sudden withdrawal of my support would take such a toll on Gato.

I arrived at the Ceiba late one evening. The sun was going down and the wind blew through the palm trees, drawing the sweet scent of coconuts from the branches to my nose. I jumped off the bus and ran over to the stairs in front of the church. Seeing Gato, who had already been drinking, I approached him, said hi, and asked if he had seen Oso.

He mumbled something, and I bent down closer to hear him. His head jerked up angrily, and his eyes glowered. "You don't love me anymore. I see how it is with you. You only talk about Oso, and you don't even ask how I am."

"Hey, that's not true. Of course I love you."

"No, Kylla ... before you always wanted to be with me, talk to me. You asked about me, and now you don't even greet me; you jump straight to questions about Oso. I'm not stupid. I realize I'm no longer important for you. And that's cool, but stop telling me you love me and then treat me like you do."

He bit his lip and fought back tears. The little boy was back, and I had hurt him unbearably. He had been betrayed by someone who had come into his life and pledged her love to him. Seeing him like this was like feeling a knife jabbed in my heart. I sat down next to him, bleeding, as he choked back tears. My body actually felt weak.

I knew I had hurt his pride. After all, I had always sought him out, and now I didn't. I knew he was jealous of the attention I had been showering on Oso and others. I even knew his words and behavior that night could have been manipulative to a degree to get my attention back, to change the current situation, to get his way. I knew all of that, but pushing aside what would have been easy to focus on, the overruling truth came to light. I *had* done what he had said. I had turned my back on him. I had forgotten that relationship was more important than numbers of conversions. I had forsaken him to impress others. Yet, still this hideous need arose in me, and I felt compelled to defend myself.

"I ask about you. You can't say I don't. It's just that Oso has been going to church with me, and I needed to ask him something. But I *am* here for you."

He leaned back against the step and shook his head. His body trembled for a second, before he spoke with a shaken voice.

"Kylla, don't lie. You and I both know the truth. You are not here for me, you are here for Oso. You have forgotten me."

"Gato, no. It's not like that."

"Right. Do you think that we don't all talk to each other? I *know* you haven't asked about me in weeks. You can say whatever you want, but I know the truth, and I'm not dumb, okay. Please remember you're a Christian, and stop lying."

He put his head between his legs, and I could hear his breathing. And then I could no longer deny the truth. It was staring me in the face. I just sat there, convicted of what I had done. I couldn't move, and I couldn't defend myself. He was right, and he was the only one brave enough to call me out. I respected him more in that moment than I ever had.

"Gato, please, look at me. I need to tell you something … please."

He didn't move. I touched his leg and continued to whisper to him to please listen to what I had to say. When he looked up, his eyes were red. He wiped away the stubborn tear he hadn't been able to keep from falling. He looked at me with a challenge in his eyes. He was vulnerable, and I knew that made him uncomfortable. He didn't know why he was even listening to me. I could see that. He was fighting against his own well-honed defense mechanisms.

"You're right. I betrayed you, because I said I loved you, and then, for weeks, I have rejected you. I don't have an excuse for my behavior, except to say I acted immaturely. I've been listening to other people who really don't understand our relationship. I wanted to be accepted in the church community more as a 'good missionary,' and I rejected you to do that. And I was wrong. Please forgive me, because I can't really imagine my life without you in it. Forgive me, please, Gatito, forgive me for being a bad friend."

"Do you really love me, Kylla?"

At that point, I could only nod emphatically. The whole exchange took more than two hours between the tears and the painful pauses, and I was questioning everything about what I was doing in El Salvador during the quiet moments when we were trying to voice what was inside ourselves.

When I thought of Jesus, I recognized he was not obsessed with numbers or with impressing people. I was ashamed of myself for how quickly I had become that which I had always despised—a measurer of people, a judge as to their worth. How far away was I from God at that moment? I didn't even know, and it took a gang member kid to hold the mirror up to my face.

My heart ached for Gato that night. My heart also ached for myself. He and I weren't so different from each other after all. I thought that God had called me to minister to him, and it seemed he had really called Gato to minister to me. That moment with him altered the rest of my time in El Salvador. I began to stop caring about the end product. I stopped obsessing about how many people I might have helped, and I began loving, truly loving, those around me, without needing so much in return.

Chapter 33

He was sitting on the curb off to the side of Plaza Barrios. He was filthy and frightfully thin. When Samuel and I passed by, he was babbling to himself. He wasn't making much sense, but his groans and gibberish seemed to call to me. I couldn't keep walking. I stopped a few feet away from him and turned around.

Samuel and I had been on our way to Mejicanos with some clothes for the gang members there. Normally I would have kept walking because this boy was not so out of place. I had seen many like him, but I remembered the conversation I had had with Gato earlier that week, and I had to stop. The boy's clothes were torn and two sizes too small. I reached into the bag I held and pulled out a pair of pants and a shirt. I handed them to him, and he hurriedly pulled them on over his tattered clothes. Samuel realized I was no longer trailing behind him and had turned around to find me.

I sat down on the curb next to the grimy boy. The people on the street now had two obstacles to step over. I heard the irritation in their voices as they went around us. Putting my arm around the boy, I introduced myself. He told me his name was Carlos. He said he was five years old.

Carlos had facial hair and appeared to be at least

sixteen. His mind was closer to the age he had told me though; he seemed to have some level of mental retardation. He might have had other disorders as well—the constant twitch, the compulsive need to count his fingers and hit his shoulder. I wasn't sure; we just sat there quietly for a moment.

It was chilly that evening in San Salvador. The temperature had cooled tremendously after the evening rain. Carlos shivered under my arm. Glancing across the street, I saw a lady selling something that looked like soup. I asked Carlos to come with me and told him I was going to give him something to eat. Taking his dirt-encrusted hand in mine, I led him across the street.

Samuel went to buy sweet bread for Carlos, and he came back with a sack full of breads. He handed it to Carlos, who promptly stuffed the bread into his mouth using both his hands. Some breadcrumbs flew into his hair and some stuck to his dry lips and sticky face. He started to cough. The bread was dry, and he needed something to drink.

Fortunately, the lady I had supposed to be selling soup was actually selling a drink called "chuco." It was a warm, filling drink, a typical Salvadoran treat. We bought a glass of it for Carlos. He would have downed the drink in a moment had it not burned his lips. He sipped it slowly as I talked to him.

I asked him where he lived, and he pointed to the city at large. I asked him where he slept, and he answered that he liked grass. He tried to find some patches of it at night. I asked him where his family was, and he resumed his humming and rocking. He requested more bread, so Samuel went to buy more.

Carlos began to play childishly with my hand. He laughed as we compared our skin color. Putting my hand to his chest, he rocked again. The sounds of San Salvador faded around us as the sun disappeared behind the cathedral that was still under construction.

A policeman approached us from behind and sternly inquired if I was okay. I'm sure Carlos and I were quite the sight, sitting and rocking on the out-skirts of the park at sundown. I assured the policeman I was not a captive or being hurt, and I thanked him for checking on me. He walked away, and I heard him make a derisive comment to his partner, questioning my worth as a woman.

While trying to pull some of the filth out of Car-los's hair as his head rested on my shoulder, I managed to get some of the breadcrumbs out. I continued to question Carlos about his life, his future, his family. I got very little information, and I realized I was wast-ing our time together really. Carlos didn't expect to be saved from his life any more than I had the ability to save him. He just wanted to rock and be close to someone. As soon as I realized that, my body relaxed and we hummed together, our song filling the night sky and giving us some peace.

Chapter 34

Tiny was just that. She was 18th Street and had been for several years, despite living in a zone dominated by Salvatrucha. She had a baby named Jamie. She liked the name; it was American, and she thought it was special. I talked to Tiny whenever I saw her. She was careful to speak proper Spanish to me, instead of the gang slang that was so common, because she wanted me to understand what she said.

I played with Jamie and paid her mother compliments about how sweet and cute she was. Tiny and I got along, even though she had to defend her conversations with me to the other girls. I had not broken the ice there, and they were not impressed.

One day, Tiny and I were discussing one of the vendors in the park who had diabetes. I had brought medicine and a blood-sugar monitor for her. Tiny wanted to see it all, and she seemed to know about the medicines. I wondered silently if Tiny could have been a doctor had she continued her education instead of running the streets.

Hammer and Ghost interrupted us, their excitement and agitation breaking in with a fierce intensity. They were warriors, and the victim had just walked into the park. They needed Jamie to help carry out their brutal task. Tiny asked where they were taking her, and Hammer pointed to the left. With that, Tiny stood up and nonchalantly handed her baby girl to Ghost. Hammer unsheathed her knife and stuck it inside the baby's blanket, hiding it from view. Hammer cooed to Jamie like an adoring aunt and her surrogate mother, Ghost, rocked her gingerly as they moved toward the victim.

I asked Tiny why they needed the baby. She patiently explained to me that the police and victim would be less suspicious of the girls if a baby were present. After all, who would kill someone in front of a baby?

My stomach knotted as the two girls crossed the street, whispering to and kissing Jamie, a sinisterly dysfunctional family. Tiny watched until they turned the corner and were gone. I didn't know what to say. I felt sick. I didn't know that the baby was gang property too. I had said that part out loud and Tiny answered with a grin, "Jamie will soon have a gang name. She's an 18th Street baby."

Her smile and pride made me shiver, and I told her I needed to go visit the vendor. The truth was I couldn't continue sitting there having a normal conversation knowing what I knew. Tiny said she'd let me know how things turned out. I walked away and wondered how many deaths Jamie would have to witness before she turned one.

The rest of my day was a blur as I rambled through Centro. I detoured for a moment to what I named the "Street of Broken Lives" to look for the man who ate the weekly mangoes I supplied him. I needed a moment on the street, to crouch down next to him, and be silent while he ate. I needed to process what I had witnessed with Jamie. I handed my friend the mangoes and squatted next to him on the filthy sidewalk.

He couldn't see the disgusted stares or the revulsion painted on their faces as they walked around him on that heavily trafficked street. He just sat with a can between his legs, hoping to make enough begging to eat.

He was covered with sores. His head, face, neck, hands, and feet were barely an outline beneath the open sores that consumed him. The gnats he had long since stopped batting away now swarmed him.

Little children cried when they saw him, and mothers hurried them along past the leprous man who lived on the corner. Nobody talked to him. The sight was almost too much to bear. He sat and closed his sightless eyes.

A few yards from him sat a large woman who lacked an arm and leg. She sweated and was dirty. Her five-year-old daughter sat on her ample lap and begged for them both. Several feet from the ragged mother and child sat a blind man, hands outstretched, asking for food or drink or anything at all.

Across the street on the opposite corner sat a woman who was deaf, blind, and crippled. She didn't have a daughter to keep her company. Her tin cup stayed in her hand. It was safer there. She would not share her pathetic wages with the world. The man who had lost both his legs in the war was propped up on a pillow a few feet from the blind lady. He begged and received sympathy from other veterans of the country's long civil war.

There were others. Some made their way to this street of misery just for the company of people like them. This battered, begging contingent lined the street, draining those who passed through of money and compassion. When the sun took its position directly over the despairing street, its patrons walked, hobbled, or crawled to a different shaded location to set up shop. The street of broken lives changed addresses, but the shattered individuals who made it what it was stayed the same.

People stared at me like I was crazy for sitting next to him. But I felt like him in that moment, helpless and scarred, just attempting to find some comfort and peace in a world that was out of our control. After twenty minutes, my legs were sore from squatting near him. Thanking him, I stood up and decided to go home.

Chapter 35

I received a phone call early one morning while preparing the bus drivers' coffee. Oso's lawyer called me and asked me to come to the local jail. Actually, I had no idea who she was talking about when she told me "Luis" wanted me to visit him in jail. She was a lawyer, and he had given her my number to use for his one phone call. After much confusion of me telling her I knew no Luis, and her telling me I must since she had called my number, I asked her what Luis's nickname was. When she said "Oso," I reassured her I would be right down. He and two other Salvatrucha members had been picked up that morning on illegal possession of weapons. I stopped by Gato's house and informed him the boys were in jail. He agreed to meet me at the jail within the hour, and when I stepped off the bus outside the jail, I saw him.

"Look, I'm going to buy them food, but you have to go give it to them. I can't go in there, or they'll stick me in the cell with them," he told me.

Gato ordered three plates of food the woman at the shack was making. I'd been told family members typically provide food and toiletries because the jail had neither the resources nor desire to do so. Gato wanted to do his part for his homeboys. As he paid for the food, he insisted to me that the police were always making up reasons to throw them in jail.

"Yeah, but you guys are gang members; do you think they're innocent of everything?"

"No, but Kylla, if we do something, okay, it's fine if they arrest us. But when they make stuff up ... that isn't right. Here, take it."

He handed me the plates of food and then wished me luck as I entered the jail. Then he boarded a bus and went into town.

I walked tentatively into the freshly painted building and was greeted by three officers with machine guns. I asked to visit Oso. The lady behind the desk eyed me and, with a sneer, told me I'd have to wait until visiting hours. When I sat down to wait the last fifteen minutes before visitation, the machine gun toting officers began lecturing about the criminals I was about to see. They showed me the makeshift guns and patronizingly illustrated how to use them. They claimed I should just go home because the gang members were guilty, and I was wasting my time.

An old man hobbled into the jail selling warm loaves of sweet bread. I bought two loaves as the lady behind the counter took up a collection from the officers and purchased a loaf herself. She told me I could go in, but she checked my bag for weapons first. She went through the toothbrushes and toothpaste, toilet paper, food, and magazines, deciding that they couldn't have the magazines because they were a fire hazard. I suspected she wanted to look at them herself, which she did.

When I entered the recently cleaned, damp, holding cell area, I heard a voice speak to me in English.

He was one of the bus drivers I took coffee to daily. Other drivers had told me that Gringo was in jail for rape. In the dank cell, he sat and told me hello. I asked him why he had done it, and his answer was short. He didn't know why. I reproached him instead of being kind. My voice rose like the officers' voices had with me. What he had done made me sick, but I couldn't help feeling bad for him sitting in this third-world jail. Softening, I gave him a loaf of bread and told him that God loved him and that he needed to change his life. He thanked me humbly and shared his bread with the other two men who shared the six-by-six cell.

I noticed Oso peering out from behind the bars. He greeted me, and I took his hand. He introduced me to Stripe and Sharky, who shared his cell and his sentence. They pleaded with me to believe in their innocence, and I passed them their bag of supplies. They were most thankful for the toothbrushes.

A small moat divided me from the cell bars. They had to relieve themselves there. The jailers cleaned it twice a day, right before visiting times. I asked what they ate, and they half-jokingly said it was beans and cockroaches instead of the customary rice. The laughter we shared brought one of the officers to the door. He glared, and I turned back to the boys, assuring them I would contact their families and friends to let them know where they were.

I began to tell them the story of Rumpelstiltskin, having just finished perfecting the Spanish rendition for the students in my English classes. I was proud of myself for my translating abilities and wanted to share my success. Sharky and Stripe looked a little bored, and Oso got nervous, since he had been the one to call me and knew he would be harassed by the others if I was an embarrassment. I didn't care, so I continued. As my voice became more and more animated, the gang members laughed and stared at me with the wide-eyed innocence of children.

When the queen was on her final guess for Rumpelstiltskin's name, I looked around and realized that every man in every cell, the officers with machine guns, the cleaning lady, the two men digging trenches to enlarge the jail, and the other visitors were watching me, listening intently to the children's story with a naivete that only comes from a lack of a childhood.

As I finished the rousing fairytale, the jail broke into applause. Sharky and Stripe begged for another story. Oso kissed my hand, and the English-speaking driver congratulated me on a story well told. The lady from behind the counter announced that visiting time was over. She had let me stay an extra thirty minutes. She liked the magazines. I let the boys know I'd be back in the afternoon, and I left, shaking my head and laughing about the absurdity of Rumpelstiltskin behind bars.

When Gato met me later that day, he asked me how the guys were. I told him they were fine, and I was preparing another children's story to tell them later that day.

"A story?"

"Well, yes. The guys are bored in jail, and I thought

it would be nice if I had something to tell them," I answered innocently.

"Kylla, I just don't know what planet you're from. It is weird that you are telling children's stories to gangsters. But it makes me laugh, so that's cool, Loca. We'll miss you when you leave."

"I'm going to miss you all too. But now I have to go teach. I'll see you later, Gatito."

"See ya."

Chapter 36

When Snake crossed the street in her baggy jeans eating an apple, she looked like a seventh grader. Her hair was always pulled back in a ponytail, and she wore no makeup. She looked like the girl next door—short, cute, and totally innocent.

She had jumped into 18th Street because she wanted to have fun. She was planning on getting out by the time she was twenty-one years old. She said she would be serious and finish school at that juncture, but now she wanted to have fun. She was young, just seventeen, and tired of her mom's rules.

Out of all the gang girls, she was the least menacing. She laughed and joked, and seemed to keep herself pretty clean, despite the partying of which she was a part. I was hoping she was innocent. I was hoping that someone I met in the gang would be a periphery player and nothing more. It was a foolish hope.

Snake killed her first MS member by jumping off a wall onto the guy's back. With her knife, she stabbed him repeatedly in the neck until he died. I talked to her the day after it happened. She was eating mangoes and drinking some juice. I said hello, and we talked.

We actually talked about everything but the murder. I knew she wouldn't admit anything to me, since I was an outsider, and I didn't want to let her know that I knew.

Snake was lucid and calm. She offered me a mango and asked how some mutual friends were doing. She looked innocent and unchanged. I felt that if I mentioned murder, she would tell me it was a mistake, that she didn't do those things. It was incomprehensible to me that she could have done something like that.

Cactus and Hammer strolled over to where we were and shook Snake's hand, congratulating her on the step up she had made in the gang. She smiled, obviously proud, and then her eyes went dead.

She looked hard and stiff. Her voice went from giddy to rough, and she talked to Cactus in hushed tones about her next chance to prove herself. Cactus seemed pleased and told her it would come soon enough. Maniaco would let her know what her orders were.

Cactus and Hammer left, and Snake looked at me again and smiled. She gave me more mango, as if the conversation she had just had had never happened. We finished our talk, and I left the park.

Snake killed two more rival gang members the same way. She was too short to approach them from the ground, so she had to jump off walls to get to them. Her reputation was growing, and she liked it. She was becoming hardened and experienced. The Salvatrucha hated her and wanted her dead.

Snake had other plans. She wanted money and knew that the fastest way to make it was to sell drugs. She hooked up with Chino, who was quite the entrepreneur. Chino was rough, and being OG didn't help his attitude. He explained the rules to Snake. Basically,

Snake would do the dirty work, and Chino would get ninety percent of all the profits. Snake agreed.

Snake took to her new job as well as she had to killing. Whenever I saw her, I asked about her original plan to leave the gang by the time she turned twenty-one. She laughed me off and told me she was having fun in her crazy life. She said she'd get out when it ceased to be fun. She assured me she knew what she was doing.

I wished her luck before I returned to the United States. I told her I would pray that she'd get out soon, that she'd return to her Christian mother, and that she'd find peace. She smiled and bit into her apple. That was the last time I saw her.

Snake messed up a few drug deals. A few buyers didn't give her the money they owed. When she had tried to explain to Chino, he had shot her in the head. She was eighteen.

Chapter 37

"Hi, Gatito. Look, I started working with the gluesniffers behind Parque Libertad. Since you were interested in those two street kids from before, I thought I'd tell you."

"That's good. It would be better if you weren't in 18th Street territory, but helping those kids is a good thing."

Gato and I were hanging out again in the Ceiba. I felt excessively tired but joyful in that exhaustion. My day always started early making coffee for the bus drivers, teaching my classes, and then getting on a bus to sweep up trash, visit gang members, street people, and now, the gluesniffers. I arrived at my house late each night, fatigued from the heat, pollution, and stress of what I saw, but ecstatic over the fact that none of what I was doing in El Salvador was planned, yet it was all so fulfilling. God had slowly but surely increased my duties in the country, never overwhelming me, giving me just enough energy to do the work.

I had a day off and decided to spend my time with the boys in the Ceiba, soaking in the shade of the tree and the tall tales that were always being told.

Gato bought me a Coke when I turned down the hot dog he offered. He stretched out next to me and closed his eyes. A teacher at my school had told me he had been in the Ceiba a week before waiting for a bus home, when he had overheard the gang members mocking me and disrespecting me. He said Gato had been the most disrespectful. I didn't really believe all of the teacher's report, but I was curious to know what had happened, so I asked Gato.

"Gato, someone told me that you guys here in the Ceiba alway make fun of me. I don't really ca—"

He jolted up and angrily interrupted me. "Who told you that?"

I was startled by his fierceness. "A guy, but I just wanted to say that I didn't care and that I'd still keep coming to the Ceiba even if people are talking. What I wanted to know is if there is anything I was doing that was offensive, so I could change it."

"It was the PE teacher in your school, right?"

I hesitated for a moment before answering. Gato was livid and completely ignoring what I was saying. Yet he had never demanded anything of me, and I felt compelled to answer.

"Yes, but chill out, Gatito. I just wanted to know."

Gato stood up and flashed some signs at a bus passing by and looked down at me as I remained stretched out on the bench.

"He showed up here to eat pupusas, and he was talking crap about you. He said that you were ridiculous, and he asked how many of us had slept with you. In the beginning, we were talking to him because we thought he was your friend, but then when he started with all of that, I told the other guys to stop talking to him."

"Oh."

"I'll just kill him. He doesn't deserve to live."

"*No,* Gato … it doesn't even matter. He's just dumb. People talk; it isn't anything new. I just wanted to know, and now I know."

"Do you believe me?"

"If you say that's what happened, that's what happened. But let's change the subject. He doesn't deserve to die, but neither does he deserve to dominate our conversation."

Gato sat down next to me after a few minutes of annoyed pacing back and forth. I decided I would share my stories about the gluesniffers with him. He humored me as I began. I started with the day I met Mama.

The rusted, battered, perpetually soiled pots and pans formed the wall of her outdoor kitchen. Colorful plastic bags were stuffed into the open spaces between the dishes, not allowing for any more light than necessary. On the makeshift door hung a grease-stained poster of a baby, a poem about love, and two pictures of the Virgin Mary. They were her keepsakes, and the Virgin was her protector.

A chain-link fence served as a window to the outside. Pots and pans, purchased at swap meets, the downtown market, or brought from home, pushed against the fence, at times obscuring her view. Utensils fell to the floor whenever she turned this way or that. Her kitchen was small, and the graveyard of chipped and bent dishes overwhelmed the provisional counters. Her shack was behind Parque Libertad—18th Street territory.

Her kitchen was a place of warmth despite the army of flies that covered the food, floor, and flimsy table. She stood with a newspaper in hand, shooing flies from her kitchen, knowing full well they would never leave. The flies were the victors, but the woman did her best.

To the gluesniffers, she was known as Mama. Fifty of her "children" came to her daily to be spoken to as a mother should speak to her child. She couldn't feed them all. She had nothing but what the Virgin had given her. She said that God would pay her later.

I met Mama when I was covered with gluesniffers, all vying for my attention and the ice cream cones I'd bought. The kids asked for a meal and pointed to Mama. I walked over to the ramshackle kitchen and introduced myself. We talked, and she agreed to make food for her children at sixty cents a plate. We shook hands on it, and she told me God would pay me. I told her he already had.

Mama began to pour the rice into big vats of oil and lard. She fried up meat and made the Kool-Aid I had with me. The line of gluesniffers grew, and their stomachs grumbled and heads ached. Mama told me to entertain them until the food was ready.

Some of the kids said they wanted to travel, so we acted like we were on an airplane, flying to exotic locations. When we landed the imaginary plane, I twisted my lips to look like fish lips. The kids laughed and tried to follow suit. Those who were successful were applauded as heroes, while those who couldn't quite do it were mocked until they quit. The kids told me jokes they never finished because too many hits of the glue had knocked the punchline from their memories. We thumb-wrestled, and they laughed when my thumb overtook their own.

When Mama announced the food was ready, a near riot broke out as they fought for position in line. It was a survival instinct. The food had run out so many times before in their young lives that they didn't know why this time should be any different. The bones jutting out of their bodies testified to that.

As Mama handed out the plates of food, they devoured it before they received their cups of Kool-Aid. I left as they fought over leftovers and the remaining Kool-Aid that barely covered the bottom of the washtub. They didn't know I had gone. The bags of glue were their dessert.

Mama and I made a deal, and weekly, we fed the children. It was all I could do, even though it wasn't enough. Mama comforted me, and I allowed her to half-convince me that what I was doing was substantial, even though neither of us could fully swallow the lie that what we did really mattered. On one such day, after greeting Mama and spotting one gluesniffer who ran back to the far corners of the lot and returned with fifty kids of all ages and shapes, I witnessed something rather strange.

She was sixteen but looked thirty. Her leg was deformed, and she walked with a limp. Her body was strangely fat compared to the other gluesniffers. I was struck by how she made a point of saying hello and thank you for the food she received. She was sweet, and in the midst of hardness and chaos, she was soft and civil.

The other gluesniffers were kind to her, letting her move to the start of the food line, making sure she had been given Kool-Aid, sharing their food with her. I didn't understand why she was different, why no one was cutthroat with her. I didn't know until it was too late.

I sat with her one day, and she told me she was very sick and asked if I could help her. I asked her how she was sick, and she didn't say. I didn't know if she knew or not. She kept saying that someone needed to take care of her, a third person she spoke of frequently. She wept that day and told me that Jesus was someone she'd like to know. She had looked at a tract that featured a small, homeless beaten boy who had died and gone to heaven. She said it was she. She wept and coughed and wept.

The other gluesniffers offered her glue, and she took some. They couldn't bear the tears. They were evidence of a truth they didn't want to acknowledge or, perhaps, couldn't acknowledge. There was pain, and life meant pain and early death.

I looked for her the next week, and she wasn't there. I asked for her, and no one answered. Shoulders shrugged, and they asked me for food. I asked Mama, and she started to cry. The girl had died giving birth to her baby. She had had AIDS, and the complications had been too much to handle.

The baby was at the hospital in ICU, and they were deciding what to do with her if she lived. The baby was HIV positive, and the doctors were not optimistic. The brain damage from the glue her mother had sniffed was extensive. There wasn't much hope.

The father of the child was a gaunt little boy around thirteen. He said it was sad that his girlfriend was dead, but that she was the one with AIDS and not him. It was life, and life was pain, so he inhaled his painkiller and stopped thinking about it. Mama fixed their food, and I left early, too tired to play in the addicts' playground.

"Life for those people in the street is hard."

Gato had disrupted my reminiscing for a moment. I kept my eyes closed and let the breeze blowing from the tree soothe my sunburned face. I had gone to the beach to visit my friend, Wende, and when I had come back, the bus drivers had made fun of me for looking like a lobster. I responded to Gato's pronouncement with an "um hum" and continued my stories.

Indio was one of them—a gluesniffer. He was an older one, a survivor of the streets. Perhaps it was the three sixes tattooed on his forehead that gave him his fearsome appearance. Maybe it was just that he was sixteen, and the height and weight that accompany puberty made him formidable. Whatever it was, he had survived. The glue had not driven him mad or to the grave.

He was brusque with the younger ones. They moved out of his way. He tended to eat first and leave before anyone could bother him. He begged for money, not in the overpopulated park but on the street I walked to arrive at my final bus depot before going home.

He greeted me every day. He remembered me, and while never maintaining eye contact, he asked me for a cólon. I paid him as if it were my toll on a freeway. I knew the money would probably go to glue, but I hoped he'd eat something too. His ribs were not visible to the eye, so I knew he ate sometimes. He had survived, after all.

Indio's eyes were wild, dancing, and empty. He never looked at me for long. His eyes darted over my head, to the left, to the right, to the ground. It was a complicated dance, as if he were being chased by the demons he had met in his life.

He tended to be wounded when I paid him for his greeting—a busted lip, a bloody nose, a cut eye, a gash in the arm, or an open sore on his stomach. When I asked him about an injury, he said he had been robbed or owed money or had been in a fight. Sometimes he said he didn't know what I was talking about. I pointed directly to a bloody gash, and he ignored me. Often, he'd start a sentence, and as if forced to leave and follow the dance his eyes started, he'd walk away without finishing the thought.

One day, Jorge, a student, was with me as we made our way back from having visited the new home of some former students of mine. When I turned the corner and began the walk down that street to the bus depot, we passed the empty stalls that typically held gumballs, mints, and bags of water. As we neared the bus depot, I heard a voice yelling crude, amorous intentions. I kept walking. Suddenly a hand grabbed my arm and jerked me back to the dark, empty stall. He repeated his intentions, as if daring someone to stop him. His seedy friend grinned.

I tried to pull away and continue my journey, but his grip was firm. I yelled to Jorge to go and get one of the bus drivers. Jorge was young and scared; he stood staring at me, unable to move. The man who held my arm was unshaven and drunk. His breath turned my stomach, and my mind raced through my options. Would I be able to fight both him and his friend off and protect my companion from seeing something so vile? I yelled to the boy again to get a bus driver to help. He had started to move, when from the right, a raggedly dressed, haggard form came running across the street, sending buses and cars careening and horns honking.

In one synchronized move, Indio hit the man's hand and grabbed me, tugging me toward the bus stop. The drunken friends were stunned as much as my companion and I. Indio dragged me to the end of the road before he stopped and put out his hand. His eyes began the maddening dance that never stopped, and I dug into my bag for two cólones. I paid him, thanking him, and before I had finished my sentence, the dance drew him back to the other side of the street and away from me.

Gato was sitting up as I finished that story. "Why didn't you tell me someone tried to rape you?"

"I had never seen those guys before or after, so I was just happy that nothing happened to me."

"You shouldn't be in the street at night."

"It happened in the middle of the day, *Dad*. Maybe I should just spend all of my days locked up."

"Shut up, Kylla," he stammered, attempting to control his laughter.

"Do you want to hear another story of how lucky I am?"

He nodded and yawned, closing his eyes, ready to rest and listen. I grinned as I watched him. He was such a dork, and I loved him very much. I relaxed again, shut my eyes, and began to tell him another story.

Sometimes things didn't work out as planned. I received a large shipment of clothes that were to be distributed among the gluesniffers. I was excited about the prospect of giving them something newer to wear. There were shirts, pants, shorts, and even some shoes.

I gathered the clothes into a big bag and headed out to the park. I saw one of my favorite kids right away. I gave him a shirt and pants. He thanked me and ran off behind the shacks, past Mama's dilapidated kitchen. No sooner had he disappeared than a huge group of kids appeared and surrounded me.

I asked them to get in line, but they fought each other instead. They ripped the bag out of my hands and pulled and tore articles of clothing away from each other. They beat each other in the street over shirts and shorts that were now tattered or stained. Chaos reigned.

Ones who were unsuccessful in their fights for clothes screamed at me. They said I was unfair, that I loved the others more, that I was rich and should buy them all things. One spit at the ground where I stood. He was angry. A girl cried. She had lost her battle for a pair of shoes.

The people in the park stopped and stared. They shook their heads at me. A few laughed, more at my stupidity than at the heinous scene they witnessed. I stood silent, unable to halt the torrent of rage around me.

The gluesniffers fought with an amazing viciousness and strength. I hadn't witnessed such passion even in gang wars I'd seen. Their strength came from the silent desperation of addiction. They saw the clothes, not as I had intended, but as a way to make money, a way to buy more of their precious glue.

It dawned on me, as I stood there, that the clothes would never be worn by these gluesniffers. They planned to sell the clothes to anyone for a cólon or two. They wanted the glue, and wanted nothing to stand in their way. They would forsake shelter, food, and clothing—anything—for a few drops of the yellow poison. I wanted to cry.

Two boys, skinny and tattered, had a shirt between them. They spun about, pulling, screaming and cussing at each other. They spun right into traffic. The bus slammed on its brakes, and the driver yelled at them.

He looked over to see what had caused the interruption to his route. He saw me and cursed.

I picked up the empty, ragged bag and walked away. I was in shock and incredibly weary. I wanted to help, to give them some hope outside the glue. However, what I had given them was more glue, another chance to kill themselves on that seemingly pleasant Sunday morning.

Gato laughed heartily as I finished my story.

"You are a little dumb, Kyllita. Taking clothes to gluesniffers … now that's funny."

"Hush, Gato. I just wanted to help them, because they are so sad."

"I know, but taking them clothes … it's just funny that you thought they would really want clothes. Everything is about glue for them."

"Well, I know that now. Sometimes people have to learn from their mistakes. And now, I am going to tell you my last story about them. Don't worry, there are no clothes in this story."

"All right, I'm listening." And so I began my story.

He sat shivering that warm tropical night beneath the fluorescent glow of the streetlight. The tears had streaked the caked dirt on his face. He shivered and bled and was silent.

Around him danced the grotesque bodies of those he called family. Their faces were caked with dirt too, but their tears streamed on the inside, leaving no tracks on the brownness; the macabre masterpiece remained intact. The dancing was punctuated by wailing and fierce rage that poured from their broken and bloodied lips. Some broke from the group, vowing to seek the culprit and exact revenge.

Still he shivered, bled, and was silent. The tears kept coming, falling from his eyes, not quite knowing the path they should take. The dancers slowed their pace when they saw me, but the car's horn and the angry curses filled my ears before I could cross to the sorcerous scene on the other side of the street. Tall and painfully thin, the silent boy's friend had tried to stop traffic, almost dying in the process. I crossed the street and was caught up into their sordid reality.

I sat with the silent boy and put my arm around his skeletal frame. The silence broke, and a moan ushered from his dry lips. The dancers stopped and began bartering with each other over who would need to stop the sobs this time. The negotiations took only a few chaotic minutes, while his sobs reached a crescendo. The boy's battered brother sat next to him and gently lifted the Gerber jar of glue to his nose and told him to inhale. The sobs stopped; his heaving body rested, somnolent, drugged into submission. There would be little sobbing now.

The bewitching dance began again, agitating itself. Sporadic in nature, it didn't seem to have a beginning or end, leader or follower. Bewitching though it was, the ever-widening pool of blood forming at the boy's ankle drew my attention back to him. The vein had been cut. I took my sock off and tied it around his ankle, trying to stanch the flow of his life onto the concrete. He winced, and the elected brother gave him another sniff from the powerful jar. He calmed down. The dance had stopped once again.

In the quiet of the moment, I asked what had happened, and the group began cursing and jolting this way and that. Applause and cheers broke out among them before I could get any answers. The avengers were back from their successful search. They saw me and began assuring the passive boy that the one responsible would not hurt him again. They had taken care of him. Violent cheers and shrieks followed this statement, as they produced Gerber jars and plastic bags filled with the yellow poison from their pockets and inhaled in revelry. The boy looked at me and smiled. Then he turned his head toward the plastic bag he was offered and inhaled.

A drunken man who shared the street with them had gotten angry and thrown his bottle at the boy. No ambulance would come. The city's ambulances had been dispatched to the coast because of spring break and, besides, this was just a gluesniffer. They always died on the street surrounded by a disconcerted dance troupe wailing and seeking revenge. They always died with the only medicine they knew being inhaled at necessary intervals from the Gerber jars and plastic bags they had found on the garbage heap.

A movie ended at the dilapidated downtown theater nearby, and a group of gangbangers walked out in the cocky style that comes from the knowledge that their presence strikes fear in the gut of every passerby. They stopped and offered support. Seeing me, they said hi and shook my hand. I knew them by their tags and tats, nothing more.

Ghost roughed the boy's hair and told him he'd be okay. She had seen him every day of her eight years controlling this park. Ghost was hanging all over Lobo. He must have claimed her for the night.

The 18th Street clique moved on, saying their goodbyes to us all, letting us get back to our morbid party. The sock was bloodied, and the boy seemed pale beneath his brown mask. I joined the dance, becoming one more ghostly figure moving around the boy, searching for help, trying to do something.

A small truck pulled up out of nowhere, once again halting the dance. We stood and watched as the driver grinned and laughed like he had stumbled upon a parade or comedy show instead of our motley group. His pickup was filled with beaming gluesniffers. They had found the ride to the hospital, an ambulance of sorts.

We loaded the boy into the pickup, bumping and jostling his leg until he almost passed out. The group quickly administered the painkiller, and he smiled up at them as the truck began its route. Gerber jars and plastic bags filled the air, and shouts of joy mingled with the honking horns and Latin rhythms as the boy and his band of brothers faded to black.

"You used your sock?" Gato had opened one eye and was looking at me with it, waiting for my answer.

"Yes, there was nothing else. I had to do something. The kid's fine now. I saw him in the park a couple of days ago. He has a scar, but he's okay."

"I don't understand you, Kylla."

I raised an eyebrow and looked at him inquisitively, not understanding why he had said that.

"It's just they're not worth anything here; we aren't anybody here. Why do you hang out with us? It doesn't make sense."

"Well, well, Gatito, now it is *you* who are the dumb one. Each and every one of you is worth so much to God, and I am here to show you that in any way I can."

He shook his head, inclined it forward, and whispered, "I just don't get it, and I don't think I ever will." I wanted to hug him and somehow force him to understand. I wanted to take him captive and make him see what the possibilities for his life could be and how much God loved him. I wanted to shake him free of the gang and every other wound he carried in his heart. I wanted to reprogram him, not give him a choice, and make him *get it*.

But I couldn't do that, so I just smiled and whispered, "I love you, Gato."

"Yeah."

Chapter 38

My two years in El Salvador would be ending soon. I would be returning home to Washington in a few short weeks. I was working with three cliques of gang members: two Salvatrucha and one 18th Street, feeding a group of fifty gluesniffers, sweeping up trash in Parque Libertad for the vendors who worked there, teaching English classes, and of course, still taking coffee to the bus drivers from the 21 bus route.

The bus drivers had become my best friends and family. It was an irony that I couldn't have imagined, since they were the people who had most terrified me in the beginning of my two years in El Salvador. I loved them very much and truly felt lucky to count them as my friends.

They bought me a beautiful hammock for a going-away present for me to have and keep always. A cobrador named Woodstock had slipped the secret to me a few days before they were planning to give it to me. He said I should have something to give in return, a recuerdo. He also told me not to tell the other bus drivers he had told me, because they would kill him. I agreed to be surprised.

I found out later what these guys had gone through to buy me something special. They collected money from every driver and cobrador over a two-week period until they had enough for something nice. Then they had sent a delegation of my closest friends from the bus line to shop.

The men met and went to countless shops, fighting about what I'd like. When the arguments got out of hand, they disbanded and met another day. Finally they agreed. They found a handmade hammock with the word "El Salvador" embroidered onto both sides. It was white and blue, just like the national flag. It was perfect, so they bought it. They had it wrapped in a big pink box with a huge bow.

I didn't know or even think they were planning on getting me something until Woodstock blurted it out. It was pretty spectacular that they were able to do all that behind my back. I was with them every morning and saw them every night. I rode the bus at least four times a day.

When I went down to the bus depot on my last day, I had the recuerdo I would present to the drivers. It was a picture frame filled with pictures of them doing silly things. I had also written an inscription to them. When I gave it to them, the older bus drivers read it and smiled. They patted me on the back.

The other cobradores and drivers looked at the pictures and laughed at the comical poses. They thanked me. Woodstock came over and told me it was a perfect recuerdo. I was relieved. I was disappointed that Abram no longer worked for the bus line because I had wanted to tell him thank you for all his patience in teaching me Spanish. He had taken a job with another bus line that had offered to pay him more money. Some of the pictures had him in them; the other drivers assured me that when they saw Abram they would let him know.

When I was leaving, the new bus dispatcher, Salvador, grabbed my arm and announced he had something to present to me from all the drivers. He said it was given to me with much affection, and they would never forget me.

Gusano came over and gave me a huge hug. He told me he thought I'd been crazy when I first started bringing them coffee, but he now knew my heart, and he loved me. I told him I felt the same way. Panda kissed my cheek and told me thank you. We hugged, and I told him I would see him again soon. Douglas gave me a hug and told me to hurry back to El Salvador.

The bus drivers seemed embarrassed about having given me something so publicly. I knew I probably didn't say the right things to thank them. I was going to miss them. I wanted to stay with them. We just stared at each other.

After I got home and opened the gift and saw how truly exquisite the hammock was, I started to cry. I felt so undeserving of their love and friendship.

I ran back up to the depot and started hugging them. The embarrassment dissipated, and they began to smile. They all wanted to know if I was going to use it. Did I really like it? Was it pretty enough? They gave me instructions on how to pack it and care for it. They told me how to hang it. I felt warmed inside, slightly speechless, which was atypical for me, and extreme happiness at having shared so many experiences with these men.

Gato came up to me and told me he had read the inscription. He asked if I really meant it. I told him I did. He nodded his head at me and told me that was cool.

I couldn't believe I had been so scared of these men when I first moved to town. I couldn't believe I hadn't liked them. I couldn't believe I had been so blind. The inscription read:

> *I heard you guys were lucky because someone brought you coffee and sweetbread, but I know in my heart the truth.*
>
> *More than my Spanish teachers, more than my cultural instructors, more than my protectors, more than the bus drivers on the best route in El Salvador, you are my friends and my beloved brothers.*
>
> *Thank you for everything. I love you and will never forget you.*

Chapter 39

I hugged him tightly and held back the tears I felt forming in my eyes. We were in the Ceiba, the place where so much time had been spent together. "I am going to miss you so much, my Gatito. You have to promise to write me."

"Yes, I will. Take care of yourself, okay? We'll always be here for you when you return. Remember that."

"I love you, Gato."

He shook his head as his half-smile formed on his lips. If I knew anything, I knew that look... a little embarrassed, a little proud, a little mischievous.

"Kylla, look, you're a good person. You have a good heart, and I just wanted to say thanks for all you did for me."

"Gato, I don't think I did anything for you, but I do know that God has taught me a lot because of you. Thanks for that."

"Take care of yourself, and come back and see us."

"Okay."

The tears had started to flow, and I couldn't talk anymore. I didn't like to cry and normally could control it, but everything was ending, and in that moment, I felt it powerfully. I hugged Gato again and told him I would write, and then I left. I completed my good-byes with my students, the other gang members, the bus drivers, and the people in town. It was time to go. I boarded my early morning flight, looking back past the machine gun toting guards, past the hoards of people clambering for their place in line, past my friends waving goodbye to me, and said a silent adios to the stunning land and incredible people that I loved so dearly.

When I arrived back in the States, my plan was to return to El Salvador within the year. I had promised everyone that. I planned to marry Samuel, my ministry partner, and we were going to open a gang rehabilitation house.

But life is interesting and often out of the control of even the biggest control freak. Within weeks of my marriage starting, it was obvious that the end was near. I was pregnant when the verbal abuse turned into threats of physical abuse. My husband told me I would never return to El Salvador. As his wife, he wouldn't let me go; and divorced, no church would support me. Being in the USA, something had happened to him and turned him into someone I did not recognize. When my daughter Faith was three weeks old, the marriage ended. After over a year of therapy, promises, and threats, I filed for divorce.

I continued to write Gato during that difficult time in my life. I sent him a picture of Faith. I promised him I would return, even though it wouldn't be the return I'd planned for myself. I received one letter to my dozens. In it, Gato reminded me that the sewage-filled swimming pool was waiting for its favorite swimmer. He asked me how I was, if I had heard about the hurricane that had devastated Honduras and done damage in El Salvador. He told me they, the bus drivers, would always remember me.

And after four years of turmoil and joy, saving money and planning for the day, Faith and I boarded the plane to San Salvador for a short spring vacation. I wanted her to see the country that made up half of her physiology. As we flew over Guatemala on our way to El Salvador, I smiled merrily. The lush green mountains and turquoise lakes stood out even from our elevated position. The farmland with its chocolate brown soil, interrupted only by rows of emerald green vegetation, divided the land into perfect quadrants. There is something distinctive about the Central American landscape. Suffice it to say, it is breathtaking, and for those of us who have lived in it, unforgettable. The lady next to me began to weep. She hadn't been home in ten years.

I wanted to see Gato badly. I had written him a number of times with little response. But I knew our friendship would survive the absence. It had to.

I arrived on a Friday and was immediately inundated with invitations to different places. Faith and I were driven all over El Salvador and shown all the sights and changes that had happened in those four years. When I saw someone I knew from before, they said hello, told me I had gained weight, and then informed me Gato was a drunk. The order of the information never changed. I needed to see him.

I didn't get the chance until Sunday evening. I was irritated, but there wasn't a whole lot I could do about it. I ran down to his house and banged on the door. Gato's mother answered the door.

"Kylla, come in and welcome. Wilfredo has been really sad because he knows you arrived here several days ago but hadn't come to see him."

I tried to explain that I had been waylaid by my hosts. I escaped as fast as I could to come see him. After all, he was my priority.

And then I saw him. My spirit both sank and soared. His hair was longer; gone was the shaved head of a teenage gangster. His nails were long, and he was dirty. He was stretched out on a bench outside the house. His face was swollen; I assumed from so much alcohol. His eyes were open as he slept. He had passed out cold for the evening.

It took me a moment to recognize him. He no longer looked like the cocky, young gang member I loved. He looked older and sadder and like he had experienced too much of the world too soon. He snored as his mother, half-brother, aunt, and I stared at him. His mom said he was like that every night. He had become a drunk. I told them to tell him I needed to see him in the morning. I would be bringing coffee to the bus drivers as usual. He needed to meet me there. His mom assured me she would give him the message.

I was crushed that the rumors had been true. I wanted so much more for Gato. It was painful to see him drunk, passed out, and unkempt. He had always taken such pride in his appearance. It made me wonder what had happened in the four years since I had been gone.

The next morning when I saw Gato crossing the street toward the depot, my heart beat faster. The dispatcher for the bus line made a comment about me wasting my time with Gato.

"Always with that same love for Gato. He's not even worth your time anymore. Your love obviously hasn't worked; you should choose someone else to care about so much. That one is going to die by the bottle, and there's nothing you can do about it." I told him that was nonsense and ran out to hug my friend.

He hadn't showered since his drinking binge. His eyes were bloodshot, and his voice scratchy. "They told me you came by last night."

"Yeah, I saw you." He looked down, a little embarrassed that I had seen him in that condition.

"Eh, you want to go to Panda's house to watch movies today?"

"No, Gato, I can't. I have to take care of my daughter. We're going to the beach today, so I can't go out with you."

"Come on, you can bring your daughter. Let's hang out today."

"I can't today, but I want to spend one day alone with you. We can go out and you can choose where we go … my treat."

"You really want to go out in public with me?"

I smiled and touched his face.

"Do you still not get that I am here *because* of you? Of course I want to go out with you. Tomorrow, you have to be here in front of the bus depot ready to go out with me. We will spend time together without all the interruptions. But you can't be drunk or hungover, or I won't go. Give me your word you'll be sober."

"Okay, Kylla. I promise, but I want to meet your daughter today."

"Okay. I'll go get her. Give me a minute."

I went to get Faith. I had hired some trustworthy girls I had known from before to look after her during her naptimes so I could go and visit people I knew. Faith loved the attention she got from these girls. They played with her hair, held her, and told her how beautiful she was. I told Faith I had someone important for her to meet. She jumped into my arms, and we went outside.

I took Faith by the hand and led her up the hill to one of the shacks. I was anxious to see a little girl named Sandra, who helped her aunt and grandma make tortillas there. She was very short and wandered around barefoot most days. She always turned my head as she lugged a huge bucket of water on top of hers. It was as if the bucket was her favorite hat. She was rarely without it. Her job was to fill the pail with water, and because her family lacked running water, Sandra had to draw water from the town spigot and carry it back to her house. The bucket pressed down on her head, forcing deep pressure lines into her young forehead. I admired Sandra's quick smile and confident manner and was excited to see her again and see if she still had to cart the family's water.

Faith and I went inside to talk to the ladies. Gato came by within a couple of minutes, having showered and changed, and sat with me. The women from the shack gave Faith and me coffee and bread while we visited, but Faith wasn't interested since she was only two. She wanted to chase the chickens she saw running around outside.

She jumped up and giggled contentedly as she ran around. Sandra watched over her as she played. After a few minutes, Faith was holding a baby chicken by the neck. I instinctively tried to take it from her. The chick did not look happy, but Faith did. Gato just laughed. I told her not to grab the animals around the neck because she could hurt them. She said okay and then ran back outside.

We just chatted with the lady who owned the shack. She wanted to know about my marriage and divorce, why Faith didn't have blue eyes, and what I had been doing the last four years. I told her as much as I could. She informed me that men were losers, and it was better to be single anyway. I smiled and agreed with her. Gato just shook his head and rolled his eyes, which made us both laugh.

Our conversation was interrupted by Faith's crying. She was in Sandra's arms and not happy about it. I was scared she had killed a chicken, but Sandra had swept her up because she had muddied her shoes and legs while running around chasing all the farm animals she had only ever seen in books.

Sandra stuck her in the cement washbasin and dumped water all over her legs to get her clean. Faith was not amused, and never having been bathed in this way, began to wail. I tried to calm her down, and thanked Sandra and her mom for trying to clean her up. They were embarrassed that Faith was screaming like she was being killed.

After she was clean and dry, Sandra deposited her in my lap to hold while she set to work cleaning Faith's shoes. She scrubbed the little shoes and bleached them, trying to make them white again. She was having a difficult time getting the mud off, and I told her the shoes were fine, and there was no problem. She finished scrubbing them and put them to the side of the washbasin to dry while we continued to talk. They looked pretty good.

Gato had been watching the whole scene intently, not saying a word. After all, washing clothes and children was a woman's job. I had never seen a Salvadoran man do it, although I was sure the exception to the rule existed somewhere. I tried to get Faith to calm down and eat some sweet bread. She leaned her head on my shoulder, obviously worn out from the exchange.

We had all picked up our conversation from where we had left off, when Gato interrupted with a question, "Are you going to leave those shoes so dirty?" Sandra looked up at him, shocked that he was commenting on her wash job. Gato continued studying the shoes. "You need more bleach; the shoes are still dirty." He dug into his pants pocket and took out a quarter, "Sandra, go to the store and get me some bleach, all right?"

I kept talking to Sandra's mom, but she was totally ignoring me, while focusing in on Gato and the new development with the shoes. Sandra looked at her mom, back at Gato, and then took the quarter and went to the store. Gato got up and started to pour water over the shoes. Sandra's mom just kept watching him, now with her mouth slightly agape. Sandra came back and handed Gato the bleach. She sat down next to me and watched him as he washed Faith's shoes. Gato lectured the ladies as he washed the shoes. He applied a lot of bleach to them and scrubbed all the stains out of them. They looked brand new, and he let the women know that.

He put the shoes to the side to dry, and then glanced up and smiled at me. I thanked him, and he said it was nothing. Sandra and her mom eyed each other, exchanged knowing looks, and smiled.

"Well, well, Miss Kylla, you have someone who is going to take very good care of you."

"Well, my Gato has always treated me very well."

And he always had, but quite honestly in the moment, I don't think I recognized the significance of the shoe washing. I thought he was being nice. But when I have mentioned that story to other Salvadorans, their reaction has been the same as Sandra's and her mom's. They have been shocked to hear that Gato would have done such a thing, a gang member, an alcoholic, a young man who defied society, and he wasn't even my boyfriend. They acted surprised, but then explained to me that it was "un muestro de carino," or a sign of affection. And I guess it was just that—affection for me and my daughter. When I asked Gato that day why he was so particular about her shoes, he had only said he didn't want her to be walking around in ugly shoes like her mother. Then he had laughed.

Chapter 40

The next day, I left Faith with her babysitters after we ate breakfast together and watched *Toy Story* for the umpteenth time. She told me she was going to play at the park. There were swings and slides, and she was excited. I told her I had to go and talk with my friend who washed her shoes. She kissed me goodbye.

I met Gato at the depot. He had showered, was sober, and ready to go. He looked a little more like I remembered him, except his pants were not quite so baggy, his shirt not sporting a gang number, and he had hair. He rubbed his eyes as he walked across the street like he had just woken up, and the sun was offensive to him. He smiled shyly at me, and I smiled back. Seeing him made me remember all our moments together, good and bad. He was my main reason for returning, and I had missed him terribly.

"Gato, I want a picture of us. I only have a couple of pictures of you, and I want something to remember today by."

He agreed and gave my camera to one of the bus drivers on the 21 bus line. We posed in front of the depot, arms around each other, smiling and contented in the moment.

"If you're a Christian, why are you hanging out with people like this? Actually I don't think you're a Christian." A sarcastic and slightly drunken voice sounded from behind us, and I turned around to see who it was. An older man I did not know was pointing his finger at me and chastising me.

"I've watched you, in the past days, bringing coffee to these bus drivers, and now you are going out with this, this … there is no way you are a Christian."

Gato dropped his head, embarrassed. I told him to lift his head up, and then I turned to the man.

"Brother, the Bible I read says we should love everyone and that I shouldn't judge people based on social status or wealth. So the Bible I read goes against what you are saying right now. You see, God told me a long time ago to serve and love *these* people … the bus drivers and the gang members, and this guy here is my friend, and I love him. You are entitled to your opinion, but I am going to do what God told me to do."

The bus drivers who were at the bus depot just listened to me, and some even cocked their heads in disbelief. Gato kicked some dirt on the ground. The bus pulled up, and we boarded. The drunken man stuck his head inside the bus and asked me why I would spend time with such people.

"It's the same reason I would spend time with you; you are important to God. God bless you, brother."

He grabbed my arm and begged me to get off the bus, to not dishonor myself by going someplace in public with Gato. I tried to get my arm free, but Gato had to help me release the man's grip. The bus pulled out, and Gato hung his head low.

"What's wrong, Gatito?"

"I don't know why that guy had to say that."

"Don't worry about it, Loco. We are going to spend the afternoon together and have a great time. I'm excited. And you know I love you, right?"

He looked at me, and I squeezed his knee.

"Why did you all say all that stuff to him?"

"To that guy?" Gato nodded. "Because he needed to know that God's love is for everyone and that we are all equal before God. And besides, it bothered me that he was talking badly about you." I tried to keep from smiling, but I couldn't. Gato tried to hide his approval as well. We looked out opposite windows as we rode into town.

"So, where are we going?"

Gato told me he didn't care. I asked him if he wanted to go to Metro Centro,[44] and he nodded yes. We ended up agreeing to see some movie whose name in Spanish I did not recognize. We bought popcorn and Fanta and took our seats in the nearly empty theater. It was the first time Gato and I had gone anywhere together. We had met up at different places and hung out, but this was the first time we had set a date to actually do something purposefully.

The movie was in English with Spanish subtitles, so I didn't even have to think during it. I told Gato that was the nice thing about movies in El Salvador; I could go to them and not have to concentrate for at least a couple hours during the day. He lamented the fact that he had to read throughout the film, but that was the price to pay for good action films. It turned out to be a lovely little Jean-Claude Van Damme picture, not my usual type of movie, but it was what Gato wanted.

The first scene freaked me out. I looked at Gato and grimaced. He laughed at me. Unfortunately, it didn't get much better after that first part. It was not my genre of choice. Gato expressed amusement when I tensed up, which irritated me. He said he had never seen me scared, so it amused him that a movie could make me so uncomfortable.

We left the movie with popcorn kernels in our teeth and an inexplicable joy shared between us. I needed to get back home to see Faith after her nap, and I told Gato it was time to go. We took a taxi against Gato's economic wishes. He said I was wasting my money. On the way home, he held my hand while I talked to him.

"Gato, you're capable of being a leader. You have to start living your life the way God wants. This excessive drinking is not a life. You have leadership characteristics. You have to realize that potential. Please, sweetie, you have to stop drinking. I can't even bear the thought of you as a drunk. I believe in you with all of my heart."

"Kylla, you're always telling me the same stuff, and maybe you're right. There were these guys who listened to what I was saying to them, and they did it. Maybe I am a leader; I don't know."

"You are a lot more than a drunk, that is for sure. You aren't living the life God has for you. You have to leave this bad stuff behind and start being the best Gato you can be."

He nodded and stroked my hand with his finger. "Do you know I love you?"

And for the first time ever he answered in the affirmative in a whisper, "Yes, I know that."

I squeezed his hand as we entered Santiago Texacuango and the place where we would part company. I paid the taxi driver, and Gato and I got out. He asked when we could spend more time together. I told him we would see each other again that night. I would meet him by the depot around 7:30 after Faith was asleep and the babysitters could watch a movie and relax.

He kissed me on the cheek and then watched as I walked to the place I was staying. I turned around to look back at him, thinking he would have already turned to go, but he just stood there, hands in his pockets, watching me. I waved, and he lifted his chin in acknowledgement, both of us wishing we could suspend time and just be.

Chapter 41

The last night of the trip, I slipped out after I put Faith down to sleep. I gave the babysitters some pop and chips and rented them a movie. They were so excited to act like the teenagers they were, they told me not to pay them. I told them I would pay them the same. If I didn't have them in the house while Faith slept, I wouldn't be able to visit my friends. I met Gato up at the bus depot after I heard his whistle. We walked over and sat down on a curb near the room where I was staying.

"Do you remember that day at the basketball court when your ex took off his shirt and showed his 18th Street tattoos?"

Of course I remembered that day; it had sent the Salvatrucha members into a rage where I thought we were both going to be killed for disrespecting their territory. I had yelled for him to put the shirt back on and forget about it. Even though he was no longer a gang member, he needed to remember the tattoos on his back.

"How could I forget?"

"They were going to kill him that day. Stripe had a gun, and he was going to shoot him. But out of respect for you, they didn't do it. I went and talked to them, and since Stripe knew you from the jail visits and all, we decided not to kill him."

I just looked at Gato, remembering the day vividly in my mind's eye. I wondered how many other times I had been in danger. I decided I didn't really want to know. I just laughed.

"And now we're divorced … "

"Yeah, maybe we should have killed him."

We both laughed, and with the laughter, the pain dissipated, and we were alone again with just the freshness of the new phase of our friendship. We talked about our lives and our future plans. Gusano got off work and passed us on his way back to his house.

"Bye, Kylla. Take care of yourself and your baby. As for your ex, don't even let it bother you; you deserve better. You're cool. Thanks for all of your help. I'll see you." He hugged me and left.

"Gusano's cool … Panda too. They are good guys, but as always, you are my favorite."

"I know."

He stood up and smashed a scorpion that had made its way across the path to us. I thanked him for killing it, and he sat down with me again.

"I was trying to think of a way that Faith and I could come live here again. Maybe I could buy a little house."

I had never really wanted to leave El Salvador, having decided long ago to spend the rest of my life there. Being back in El Salvador, visiting all my friends, reminiscing with Gato, my mind raced with possibilities. Maybe I could teach again or maybe I could bring Faith back every summer and spend my vacation there. I pointed to a small house in our line of vision. Gato paused and got really quiet. He just stared ahead at the house. And then in a whisper, he said, "That would be good, Kylla. I would love it if you were here again. You make me feel good."

I begged him to leave his alcoholic life, just as he had left the gang, a fact he had shared with me earlier that day. It was like he was switching one vice for another, equally as frightening and deadly. He had to be responsible and a good example for his little brother. He shot me a look of anger and hurt, but I continued.

"You can't think that you are living a great life, Gato. You have to reflect on it all; this isn't the life you should have. I believe in you, and I trust you. You could change if you wanted to. And so I am begging you, please, change your life. I am really worried about you."

He nodded his head in agreement. We talked about other things, laughed about past times, and then he told me that Killer—Jaime—was living a Christian life. He was married with two kids. He was working and going to church every week. He wanted to see me, so he could thank me for all the times in the past when he would come and ask for help only to return to the gang again and again. I think my smile could have cracked my face. I was so happy, I hugged Gato hard. Gato just laughed. "I thought you'd like that bit of news."

"Of course, I would. How exciting. I am so happy. Thanks for letting me know."

We talked for an hour longer, then I told him I

had to go. My plane was leaving early in the morning, and I needed to sleep. We stood up, and Gato grabbed both of my hands.

"Kylla, I don't really know what to say. You are special. Thanks for all of your support. I'm going to try and change my life for you."

"Gatito, I hope you change your life; but don't do it for me, do it for yourself. It's so important. You are so important. I have felt this love for you for so many years, and it has to be for a reason. I don't know what it is, but God has a plan for you. I love you and am going to miss you so much. I promise to write you more than I did before."

He pulled my hands closer to him, which pulled my whole body into his, and as his lips pressed against mine, I kissed him back. We stood there kissing for a couple of minutes, and it was as if I were sending all of my hopes for his life to him by my kisses. As ridiculous as it may sound to some, it wasn't a romantic kiss, despite its having all the necessary components.

That moment felt different, the culmination of six years of unexplained intense feelings, mixed with the desperate longing from both of us that the moment would stay, that a great change would occur in our lives and that we wouldn't be the same people, but that we would remember everything that had transpired. I wanted him to change and begin to live. He wanted me to come back and live near him, yet we both knew they were not the most realistic of dreams. And maybe the kiss was a physical reminder of what could have been—an easier time with no complications where we could have existed together as purely as is possible.

When we stopped kissing, we stared at each other for a moment, neither of us speaking. He still held my hands, and I broke free and hugged him close to me.

"I love you, Gato."

"I love you too, Kylla."

"I gotta go."

"I know. Take care of yourself and hurry back."

"Of course I will, but you have to be here waiting for me."

"I know. Tell your daughter hi for me, and take care of her."

"Of course I will. Goodbye."

"Goodbye."

Chapter 42

When I returned from the trip, it was my twenty-ninth birthday. I felt compelled to write Gato a lot more than I had before. I must have written him fifteen or more notes within my first weeks back home. I clarified the kiss, although there was probably no reason to. We really never had viewed each other as boyfriend or girlfriend, but I felt I should explain myself to him.

I was scared for him and the alcoholism. The alcohol in El Salvador is not monitored as fervently as it is here. The liquor sold on the streets has a very high proof, and I worried that Gato would drink too much and die. So I wrote, thinking that might have some effect.

I had returned to school to get my master's degree in special education. I had a passion for working with kids with behavior and emotional problems, and I wanted to get into a classroom and help. Faith was growing up and becoming the fascinating child she is today. I was busy teaching Spanish in a small private school, going to school at night, and being a single mother in all the other moments. My own mom was helping me tremendously with school and childcare. Her advice when it came to Gato was to pray and keep writing, so I did.

I went to a friend's wedding in the summer of

2002 and reacquainted myself with one of my best friends from college. I knew I was going to marry him very soon after our friend's wedding. He was good and kind, and the type of man who could handle all of my passion and strength and the neuroses that went along with it. He knew me, and far more importantly, he loved what he knew. Faith fell in love with him, and to this day tells me she chose him, because he is "a good one." I wrote Gato to let him know.

I got married the following summer to Cory, and a month later received a letter from Gato, the second and last one I ever received. He told me he was in a rehabilitation house; he was getting better. But he had better news: he was a Christian. Now he was my real brother. He congratulated me on my wedding. He told me I deserved to be happy. He told me how happy he was for me. Then he apologized to me for not being a better letter writer, but that he always thought of me.

"Kylla, even through the distance and the time that has passed, you always were and always will be my guardian angel."

He told me he loved me and wanted me to be happy. He asked when I would return to El Salvador. He would be waiting for me with arms outstretched to give me a hug. He was my Gato, and he would be waiting.

Chapter 43

Cory helped me plan my return trip to El Salvador. He would watch Faith for me, so I could visit more people and get more accomplished. I hadn't been back in two years. I needed to see Gato. Having not heard from him in some time, but having received letters from his mother telling me he had gotten out of the rehab home but had fallen off the wagon, I felt desperate to see him. He had been in and out of the hospital due to different diseases and complications attributed to the alcohol. I was terrified. I had to go.

Cory kept telling me, as the time drew closer, that he had a bad feeling about the trip. I chocked it up to El Salvador being a developing country, and Cory's conservative nature. Nothing more, nothing less. He took me to the airport, and I kissed him and Faith goodbye.

When I arrived in El Salvador, I closed my eyes and breathed in the heat and humidity. I was happy just having set foot on this magical land. I found my ride and had people waiting to take me out as soon as I arrived. I didn't even have time to change clothes before I left for my first outing with Gato's mom and her friend. We went to Pollo Campero, where they bought me lunch.

"Gato's a drunk. It is such a shame. He has had so

many chances to change, and he just doesn't want to. He's an embarrassment."

"No," I responded defiantly, at the same time trying to be sensitive to the fact that they had lived through all of this on a daily basis, and I had not.

"It's hard to give up an addiction. He's an addict, and he's struggling. You shouldn't judge him, because it's hard. I am as disappointed as you both are. I would love to see him as a victor over all of this, and not as a drunk, but I love him, and that's not going to change."

They stopped talking about him after that. We ate our chicken and talked of other things. It was nice getting to know more people whom Gato knew and who knew Gato. I didn't know why they were so angry with him, but I also didn't want to imagine if I had lived day in and day out with an alcoholic.

The first time I saw him that trip, Gusano took me to the bus depot where Gato was working. He had quit the 21 bus line long ago and was working with Panda. Gusano chastised me the whole way to the bus depot.

"Why are you dressed like that, Kylla? You look ugly and fat, and not sexy at all."

I looked at myself in my oversized T-shirt, black exercise pants, and Teva sandals and laughed, not quite the look of a typical Salvadoran woman who always looked beautiful and ready to go out.

"What? I don't want all of the men looking at me. It's better if I walk around like this, bagged out and ugly."

"But you dress well sometimes, right? You wear heels, skirts; you look pretty sometimes still, right?"

"Well, yeah … when I go to work, I put on nice clothes, but right now I am wandering around downtown San Salvador … so … "

"At least sometimes you look pretty, because right now, you look horrible."

I just laughed, which made Gusano laugh. We were nearing the bus depot, and I was so excited to see Gato. I could barely contain myself. When we arrived, Gusano asked the dispatcher when Gato's bus would arrive. He told him I was a special visitor and wanted to see Gato. The dispatcher looked me up and down, and not being impressed, just grunted. Gusano leaned in and whispered in my ear, "I told you you should dress better, woman!"

When Gato got off his bus and saw Gusano and me, he smiled, got his notebook checked by the dispatcher, and then hurried over to talk to us. He hugged me, but then looked at me and said, "Are you pregnant? You look really fat, girl."

Gusano laughed. "I told her that too, but the crazy girl told me it was 'better to wander around bagged out so the men wouldn't look at her.'"

"She's right, because the guy would have to be crazy to think she looked good."

I slapped Gato on the shoulder and told him to shut up and we should eat breakfast together. He looked a lot different. But I tried not to pay attention to all the physical changes. I was happy to see him again. I ordered my delicious casamiento[45] and he his eggs and avocado, while Gusano ate chicken and beans next to us. We talked, and I asked him when I would be able to take him out.

"Next week. I don't have a day off this week. But maybe we could go out next Tuesday, do you want to?"

"Why yes, Tuesday is great. Now you know why I'm here, right?"

"For me."

"That's right; don't forget it."

"Never."

We finished breakfast, and Gato went back to work. I spent the day with Gusano and Panda at Panda's house. His wife made me the best pot of beans with warm tortillas while we relaxed, watched movies, and played video games. It felt nice to be back among friends, laughing and remembering old times.

"Kylla, you shouldn't be staying where you used to live. You should be here with me and my family. You should be with friends. We would do whatever was necessary to make your trip nice."

"Thanks, Panda. I appreciate that, and maybe the next time, I will stay with your family."

"That's how it should be."

We hung out for hours and had a good time. The next day, I went to take coffee to the bus drivers. So many of them were new, and I didn't know them. The old remnants laughed when they saw me and drank the coffee, commenting that they were traveling back in time to when I had lived there, and that it was good to see me.

Another friend of mine arrived, and we went and had breakfast together. Douglas had coffee while I ate, and we talked. Gato crossed the street unexpectedly; I thought he said he had to work. I was surprised to see him, but thrilled. He walked up to our table and greeted Douglas and me. Douglas whispered to me that Gato was jealous we were eating together. I grabbed Gato's hand and pulled him onto the bench and told Douglas there was no reason for Gato to be jealous. He was my favorite.

"We all know that. You don't have to keep saying it... enough already." He laughed, and I looked at Gato and told him I was happy to see him. The three of us talked and reminisced, and Gato paid for all of us just as he had when Gusano and I had eaten breakfast with him at his job. Gato asked if I would be around. I told him I had plans for the day, but I would look for him that night. He complimented me on the fact that I had worn heels and a dress.

"Finally, you look pretty. Congratulations."

"Ohh, thank you, kind sir. You are *so* sweet."

He laughed with me as I punched him in the arm for his sarcasm. I walked with him out of the diner and across the street. He accompanied me halfway to the place where I was staying.

"I'll come looking for you tonight. Wait up for me. I want to talk to you, Gatito."

"Okay."

We parted company, and I went with his mother and her friend to a birthday celebration I had planned on attending since I arrived. I got caught in the rain while trying to catch a bus back from San Salvador to Santiago Texacuango. I was soaking wet, so I ran back to where I was staying and changed clothes. I smelled like wet dog and looked horrible, but I had to get back outside and hunt down Gato. I felt an urgency to see him and just talk with him.

I couldn't deny any longer the physical changes he had undergone. He had battled hepatitis and an assortment of other ailments by this time. He had, for the better part of the past year, been in and out of the hospital fighting for his life. His voice box had been damaged the last time he had been in the hospital, when the doctors had to put tubes down his throat to help him eat or breathe or both. His voice sounded like two cats had gotten into a brawl in his throat, and he had lost. His skin and eyes were yellowed, and he was missing his front teeth, another casualty of the doctor's invasion into his throat. Now only jagged remnants remained. His skin was puffy, and he looked sick.

I ran down the road to his house. A group of guys were hanging out in front of it. I didn't know them, and I couldn't see them well because the darkness was thick like molasses. I ignored them, and they reciprocated. I banged on the little tin door that was propped up by rusty nails and a rotting wood fence. The piercingly loud barks of five dogs erupted, and any worry I had of Gato not knowing someone was at the door dissipated. After a couple of minutes, he looked out the door and saw me, wet and bedraggled. I said he had to come with me and hang out. He shook his head at me, the perpetual look of surprise and amusement on his face when I would do something that was so obviously American. But he told me to wait for him to put his shoes on. I smiled. I was so happy at that moment.

I turned around and waited. The group of guys made a joke about me. I looked at them and recognized Gato's half-brother in the group. He thought that any-one who hung out with his alcoholic brother deserved the same level of ridicule that he and his friends threw at the drunks in town. I just kept on smiling because I knew they didn't have a clue as to what Gato was about. They accepted the outward signs of a person as proof of something definitive about their character, all the while missing the person inside the shell.

Gato came out, and I asked him where he wanted to go. He asked me if I was hungry. I nodded yes. We went to eat pupusas at one of the little shacks up the road. We sat eating our pupusas and drinking our sodas, talking and laughing and staring at each other in silence. He was beautiful in his pitiful state. I was so happy he was alive. I started to ask him about the rehab center where he had spent so much time, but Gato stared silently out the window of the diner.

He motioned at someone to come in and sit with us. At first, I thought he was trying to avoid the ques-tion, but then a guy came in from the darkness and sat down. He was the mute boy who lived in town. Gato and he had developed a way to communicate. He always turned up when I was with Gato. Two years ago, the night before I was to leave for the States, this boy had shown up and talked to Gato for a time. I had been impressed with Gato's patience then. I was now impressed by the genuine friendship he and Gato shared. He asked him if he wanted some pupusas. The boy was starving and nodded his head vigorously. Gato ordered two more pupusas, but then gave the boy the one off of his plate so he could eat immediately. He ordered a Coke and gave it to the boy. Then he talked to him about the weather, the local gossip, and his plans for the week. I just kept eating. I was not privy to the intricacies of their communication system.

After he paid, Gato and I waved goodbye to the boy, who was still eating. Gato explained to him that he was going to leave and talk to me, since we hadn't seen each other in two years. The boy wished us a good evening and then finished his pupusas and bag of churros.

"I love you, man. You know that, right?" I grabbed his arm and squeezed it.

"I know," he responded in the dark and walked with me, his head held high.

I told him I wanted to know about his stay in rehab when he had written me. He told me he had asked Jesus into his heart. "For real ... not like before." He winked as we both remembered the time when my ministry partners had detained him from his breakfast to get a quick conversion from him. I laughed.

"You know what? I've missed you a lot. I've thought about you every day, and I'm so happy to have time to spend with you. I want to talk to you and just hang out with you."

"Kylla, you are crazy ... always with the conversation. I don't even know what to say."

"Well, tell me how old you are. Tell me that … it's pretty easy to answer simple questions like that. Everyone keeps telling me different ages and you, too. I'm eight years older than you, right?"

"I'm thirty-five."

"Liar!"

"No really, I'm thirty-five."

"That's a bunch of crap, man."

Gato laughed and continued his joking. "Look, an elf showed up in my dreams and asked me how old I wanted to be, and I said thirty-five."

"An elf?"

"Yeah."

"Gato, I'm not the crazy one here."

He continued to tell me about the imaginary elf who had visited his dreams. He was very animated as he told me the story. We laughed like we had in old times. He always joked around with me, trying to make me laugh and forget the seriousness of all our conversations. But as suddenly as we began laughing, we stopped and just looked at each other. I couldn't continue in our make-believe world any longer.

"You can't die, Gato. You're mine, and you can't die. You have to live longer than me. Promise me that."

"Kylla, you know I can't promise you that."

"I'm not giving you an option! Stop drinking and live your life, Gatito."

"Kylla, I'm going to die before you. You have to accept that."

"No!" I screamed. "How am I supposed to accept that? You are young, and you can live. Just try!"

He just looked at me with his sad eyes, and I stared back defiantly at him, my eyes filling with tears.

"You have to live. I don't know what I'd do without you," I whispered.

And then we were silent. He told me to come and sit next to him, and he held my hand. We sat there and let the tropical wind assault our faces. In the horror of the moment, there was calm. He had my hand, and I didn't want to let go, as if that could somehow heal him and keep him with me always.

He lifted our entwined hands to his eyes and just stared at them. I just watched him. My stomach felt sick. How would I be able to let him go? He brought our hands to his mouth and kissed mine.

"It's okay, Kylla. I've lived my nine lives ... with the ninth ... well ... you know, I'm only a cat." He smiled and tried to laugh a little. I tried to as well. It was an anemic attempt to lighten the mood.

We talked and laughed and reminisced about past times. He asked about Faith and Cory. I rested my head on his shoulder as the hours ticked by. He told me he had missed me, too. He didn't want me to leave when I told him I had to go and get some sleep. It was past midnight, and I was tired. I thought I would have more time with him later that week. I didn't know it would be the last time I would see him.

He walked me back to where I was staying. We wished each other a good night, and I gave him a hug.

"I love you, my Gato."

"I love you too, Vaga."

And he disappeared around the corner and into the night.

Chapter 44

The next night I was raped. I had gone to dinner with a supposed friend, one of the only wealthy people I knew in El Salvador. He was a business associate of newly-elected President Antonio Saca and had many friends in the legislative assembly. A powerful man, Manuel liked to talk politics, and knowing I was always ready for a good debate, he invited me to dinner.

We ate at a Chilean restaurant and had a few glasses of wine to temper our tempers. I realized while I was dining with him why most of my friends were the poor. I couldn't stomach much of what Manuel was saying. "The poor shouldn't even have the right to vote in elections. They are trash. They don't know anything, and all they know is to rob people." When I reminded him *he* had started poor, he assured me he was different, one of the only quality people left in his country.

He ended the meal by telling me my two years in El Salvador had been a waste and that God must be very disappointed in my work. "You worked with so many people, and you only had like five of them who accepted God's Word. Kylla, I don't believe you are that smart." The restaurant was closing, but I was determined to get my last few political questions answered by Manuel, since I knew I wouldn't be able to tolerate another meal like this. He told me he knew a place where we could drink some coffee and discuss politics some more—"a place with rich people."

Where he took me was far from that. When it was over, I just wanted to go home. I wanted to find Gato and tell him goodbye, but I knew he was at work, and I couldn't find the strength to search for him. I needed to go home and be with my family.

When I arrived back home, I wrote my five closest friends in El Salvador and told them what had happened; Gato was the first of the five to receive his letter. His aunt wrote me later and told me he had cried and ripped up the letter, somehow hoping to make the act disappear with the paper that was its testament. I wrote Gato every day, at least once, starting with that letter. It was cathartic for me and, I felt, necessary for him. I told him I wanted to see him well. I needed to see him living his life the way God intended. He had to change. He had to be okay.

When I received the phone call a month and a half later that he was dead, I pressed the phone to my ear and told the girl who had called to repeat herself. I wasn't really surprised, because he had been so sick and weak and had been near death so many times before, but I didn't want to believe it. Every thought ran through my mind. I should have stayed. I should have never left him. I sat for an hour in silence, not wanting to accept that it was over. Everything was over.

But when the news traveled from my brain to my heart, I could not stop crying. I felt a physical rip in my heart. I ached inside and didn't know if I could recover or if I even wanted to recover. My Gatito was dead; my El Salvador was gone. And I had never said goodbye.

I received another call from a friend of the family, telling me I should stop sending letters; they had continued receiving them after he had died. I told her they would stop, that there was a lag in the mail, and since I had written him every day, there were bound to be some letters that would still arrive.

"Throw them away; they don't matter anymore." As for me, I couldn't throw away the letter I had yet to put in the mail to him. I held onto it for months thinking that maybe it wasn't true, that he wasn't dead. But eventually, I had to let it go.

I heard that hundreds of people showed up to his funeral. My friends wrote me to tell me that Gato was loved, that people from all over El Salvador had come to pay their respects and leave roses at his tombstone.

"The people didn't even fit in the house; they had to stand in the street to say goodbye to him. He always had friends from all over the place. We didn't even know a bunch of the people who showed up. He was special, but I guess you knew that, right?"

And I did know, but I didn't know if Gato had. So often, people can't see who they really are, how special they have been created to be, how they impact others, and how their disappearance from the world can devastate so many. Perhaps Gato did not live the life he was made to live. He lived a broken life and didn't overcome it in a way that would impress others. He died an alcoholic at a very young age.

But I would say that Gato impacted more people for good than would be seen at first glance. He helped the mute boy and loved him unconditionally. He treated everyone he met with dignity and respect, even though the world had treated him horribly. He tried to help his fellow gang members find their way in this world apart from the violence and seduction of gang life.

I can still see him playing and laughing with those little gluesniffing boys. I can see him walking past the bolos in town, before he joined them, sharing his coffee and sweetbread with them. He changed me and my worldview. He was somehow able to reach into my heart and confuse me about what I thought I knew. He helped me learn to love someone unconditionally and to extend my hand without always needing something in return. And I am sure I am not the only one on whom he had an impact. Out of the hundreds of people who came to his funeral, there are bound to be others who saw through his exterior and into his heart and were changed by it.

His life is not so easily expressed. There is neither clear victory nor defeat in it. He was a gang member and a drunk to be sure, but he was also a beaten-down boy who dared to raise his head again. He died young without money or accomplishments, but he had hundreds of friends, and to those of us who knew him well, he was one of the best souls that walked the earth. He let alcohol take his life after having given into its temptation too many times. But he never stopped caring about others, expressing his humanness in daily tasks, loving when he was not loved back, and living despite so many having wanted him dead from the earliest moments of his life.

I listen to Juanes again—his new album, *Mi Sangre*—and I sing the song that is my Gato. We have now switched the role of guardian angel. I was his, and now he is mine. That is what I believe.

Duérmete pronto mi amor Que la noche ya llegó
Y cierra tus ojos que yo De tus sueños cuidaré
Siempre a tu lado estaré Y tu guardián yo seré
Toda la vida Si un día te sientes mal yo de bien te llenaré

Y aunque muy lejos tú estés Yo a tu sombra cuidaré
Siempre a tu lado estaré Y tu guardián yo seré
Toda la vida ... Duérmete mi amor, sueña con mi voz Duérmete mi amor hasta que salga el sol.[46]

Endnotes

Introduction

1 A disappeared person is someone who is taken in the middle of the night—or day, for that matter—and never heard from again. Their bodies are often never recovered.

2 Archbishop of El Salvador who was martyred on March 24, 1980, for defending the rights of the poor.

3 A town that was destroyed and its people murdered by the Salvadoran Army for appearing to be guerrilla sympathizers. Over 900 people were killed including women and children.

4 Bean soup and Salvadoran tortillas.

5 Pupusas are the typical food of El Salvador. They are bean-and-cheese-stuffed corn meal that is fried and served with a cabbage and vinegar-based salsa called cortido.

6 The Farabundo Martí National Liberation front, the guerrilla group who fought in the twelve-year civil war and is now a political party in Salvadoran politics

7 Bananas, five for a cólon (about twelve cents)

Chapter 1

8   An extremely popular Colombian rock star who sings songs of his people and, as I have found, the people of Latin America, including my Gato. The song quoted here is called "La Historia de Juan," and it is from Juanes' CD entitled *Un Dia Normal:* 440017532–2, P & C Surco Records 2002.

9   "So strong was his pain that one day it took him away. So strong was his pain that his heart gave out. So strong was his fear that one day he just cried. So strong was his fear that one day his light turned off."

10   "Juan asked for love, and the world refused him. Juan asked for honor, and the world dishonored him. Juan asked for forgiveness, and the world hurt him. Juan asked and asked, and the world never listened."

11   The crossroads between Santo Tomas and Santiago Texacuango in San Salvador.

12   A cobrador is the person who collects the bus fare for the bus driver in the bus system.

13   "He just wanted to play. He just wanted to dream. He just wanted to love, and the world forgot him."

14   "He just wanted to fly. He just wanted to sing. He just wanted to love, but the world forgot him."

Chapter 2

15   Pupusas are the national food of El Salvador. They

are corn meal filled with beans and cheese or other fillings that are fried.

16 The Ceiba was a courtyard outside the Catholic church in town. There was a large ceiba tree in the middle of the courtyard, hence the name.

17 Gang word for girlfriend.

Chapter 3

18 One of the two largest gangs in El Salvador; Mara Salvatrucha, the number 13 is associated with this gang as well as the letters MS.

Chapter 6

19 MS stands for the Mara Salvatrucha. They are used interchangeably when referring to this gang.

20 Diablo means devil.

21 Pie Grande means big foot.

22 Comeninos means child eater.

23 Vampirata is a vampire rat, and Chupacabra is a goat sucker, a mythical animal that sucks the blood of livestock.

24 Panda Oso means panda bear.

Chapter 7

25 The African National Congress was formed as a resistance group against the racially segregated

form of government known as apartheid. Nelson Mandela was one of its founders.

26 Can opener, crib, curtains, cow, chalkboard, flag, chair, bed, steak, farm, desk, bathroom, CD

27 The FMLN was the guerrilla group during the twelve-year civil war. It is now a political party. ARENA is the reigning political party. They could be loosely characterized by comparing the FMLN to ultra-liberal democrats and ARENA to ultra-conservative republicans.

Chapter 8

28 Tita's Diner

29 No, I see nothing, nothing, nothing.

Chapter 11

30 Yes, no, truth

31 Desvio is where the bus stop is located in between Santo Tomas and Santiago Texacuango.

32 Derogatory term for a member of the 18th Street gang.

Chapter 12

33 Homies, homeboys, good friends, these all mean the same thing.

Chapter 13

34 Pretty girls, precious ones.

35 Hey, pretty girl, cute white girl, come here.

Chapter 16

36 Expressed as the party life essentially…drugs, sex, rock and roll.

Chapter 18

37 "Bananas…two for a cólon. Chicken (feet) soup…five cólones. Bean pupusas…for two cólones."

Chapter 20

38 A park in downtown San Salvador that was, at this time, 18th Street gang territory.

Chapter 21

39 OG means that you originated out of Los Angeles or somewhere considered legitimate in the gang world. You also must have paid your dues and spent enough time in the gang to hold a valued position. The term automatically gave people respect on the street.

Chapter 23

40 "We are small in number but great in craziness."

41 Green light is when your own gang essentially puts a hit out on you. If you are in green light, your own gang is looking to punish or kill you.

Chapter 30

42 My crazy life. Those three words go hand in hand with gang life. Most gang members have a tattoo of them or at least talk about the crazy life all the time.

43 A fried chicken restaurant

Chapter 40

44 Metro Centro is a shopping and entertainment area similar to a mall in the United States.

Chapter 43

45 Rice and beans mixed together ... it is delicious.

Chapter 44

46 "Sleep soon, my love, because the night has already arrived. And close your eyes so I can take watch over your dreams. I will always be at your side, and I will be your guardian all through life. If one day you feel bad, I will fill you with good. And even

if you are far away, I will watch over your shadow. I will always be at your side, and I will be your guardian all through life. Sleep, my love, dream of my voice. Sleep, my love until the sun comes out." These are the words to "Tu Guardian," by Juanes from his CD *Mi Sangre,* P&C 2004 Surco Records.